Just Bones

A Mystery

by

Jeffrey Denhart

A Write Way Publishing Book

Write Way Publishing
10555 E. Dartmouth, Ste. 210
Aurora, CO 80014

First Edition; 1996

ISBN 1-885173-15-6

3 4 5 6 7 8 9 10

CHAPTER ONE

When I parked my 1956 Mercury in my garage, I was a happy man. I had driven 184 miles round trip to a car show sponsored by Sioux City's county fair. The car performed perfectly on the road, and although I didn't win, it drew several compliments. I even found a source for spare parts. I simply couldn't have had a better day, and I planned an equally pleasant evening consisting of a special sandwich from Emma's Deli, the last half of a mystery novel, and a half a pint of brandy.

The indicator light on my message machine destroyed my buoyant mood. Phone messages seldom brought good news, and I tried to pretend that I hadn't seen the light. I was successful for a few minutes while I used the bathroom and changed my shirt, but when I settled into my recliner chair in the living room, the light found its way into my field of vision from every angle. I relented and pushed the play button.

As I predicted, the message was bad news. My ex-wife had called, said it was important, and to call her back. This usually meant she needed money. Although we had been divorced for twenty years, and she had remarried twice, she was still able to manipulate me and make me feel guilty. I was never certain how she did it, she was that good at it. I knew I couldn't return the call without some mental preparation or she'd go over me like a steam roller. I usually tried to guess her reasons for thinking I should give her money, and I developed arguments against them. Even with this preparation, I expected her to win; I only wanted to put up a decent resistance.

I thought I'd have dinner before I called her in order to prolong my near-perfect day and to get some energy to argue. I was extricating myself from my recliner when my beeper went off. As usual, it made me jump. I liked beepers less than phones, but I had to have one for my job. The flashing number was familiar, and I dialed the sheriff's office.

"Yeah, Mary. Bill. What's going on?"

"Thank God you called back. Bird's been trying to get you for over an hour. Something happened by the lake. Don't you wear your beeper?"

"It's Saturday, Mary. My day off. Why are you working?"

"Bird got me in to find you. Thank God it didn't take too long. I'll patch you through."

I listened to static for a few minutes as Mary raised Bird on his radio. Bird's given name was Eugene, but I doubted if many people remembered it. He had used his nickname since he was christened it in high school for both his last name of "Starling" and his long, gangly limbs. In high school he had excelled at basketball and drag racing and spent more than one night in the jail that he had managed for the past fifteen years.

"Yeah, Bird here," his voiced crackled through the phone.

"I found Bill," said Mary. "He's on the line. Go ahead."

"Bill, listen. Get out to the lake pronto. You know that old hotel they're tearing down? Well, since it was a nice day the demolition crew decided to get an early start. They really found something."

"What, Bird?"

"I don't want to get into it on the radio. Too hard to describe. Get out here and bring your kit."

"This is work, Bird? You got a body out there?"

"In a way. Now get out here." The phone turned to static and then a dial tone as Bird terminated the conversation.

I was annoyed. I had been home only fifteen minutes and my day was spoiled by a message from my ex-wife, and now I had to work on Saturday night. Actually, since I was the county medical examiner, I could expect to work some odd hours, and I got my coveralls with ME on the back and my evidence kit from the closet. I debated briefly about wearing the coveralls, and decided against it. They were made from treated nylon to eliminate as much fiber shedding as possible, which made them unbearable in hot weather, and the temperature had hit the high nineties today. I decided to put them on at the scene. Before I left, I called Emma's Deli and ordered a special to go; at least I could have one part of my evening.

I started the five-year-old mini-van that the county provided for my use. Its belts whined and lifters ticked until the oil warmed sufficiently for lubrication. Compared to my Mercury's steering wheel, the van's was minuscule, and I oversteered the first two corners before I readjusted. I stopped for my sandwich and drove down Bishop's Main Street toward the lake that bore the same name.

Bishop was my home town, but in high school I thought of nothing except leaving its claustrophobic smallness and midwestern uniformity. The day after graduation I drove to Los Angeles where I married, had a son, divorced, graduated from USC's medical school, and worked in the emergency rooms of the county hospitals.

Twenty years of my life passed, and I was a graying, middle-aged man with bad feet and varicose veins from long hours in surgery. I lived alone in an apartment that was decorated mostly with dust, and worked double shifts sewing up the wounds of gangsters and their victims, only to see them again with new wounds, often fatal ones. My social life consisted of staff Christmas parties and occasional liaisons with nurses who were as lonely as I. I had lived half my life and had only a medical degree, a son I saw once a year, and an old car to show for my efforts. When my father died, I applied for a leave to arrange the funeral, settle his estate, and regain my perspective. I returned to California only to ship my belongings home to Bishop.

For the past four years I have lived in the house that, due to an unusually heavy snowstorm, I was actually born in. I began working in the emergency room of Bishop's county hospital, and found it unlike ER service in Los Angeles. There, I frequently performed surgery, often for gunshot wounds, for eight to ten hours at a time. Now I took care of infections, some broken bones, and an occasional heart attack. I had enough free time that I considered starting my own practice, something that I had never had. This gave me some anxiety because I have difficulty developing and maintaining relationships. I was more comfortable dealing with a person's immediate symptoms or operating on an anonymous body part than I was with providing patients the continued care they need and deserve. When Bird offered me the position of county medical examiner, it solved my quandary. I could fill my free time, supplement my income, and avoid dealing with patients. My duties as ME were as mundane as my ER service; most deaths in Bishop were caused by old age instead of violence. That same boring uniformity that repulsed me as a teenager attracted me now, and I thoroughly enjoyed the routine work demands, reading mystery novels, and tinkering with my Mercury.

It took me about twenty minutes to reach the site of the old hotel, which was on the far side of the lake. Lake Bishop itself is large: over five miles long and a mile wide at its center. For years it had fostered a modest tourist trade, which helped the economy of the town of Bis,hop. Most of the trade was seasonal, and cottages and lodges dotted the lake shore catering to families interested in swimming, fishing, and boating.

The old hotel, if it had a name it had long been forgotten, represented the first attempt to promote tourism on the lake. It had been built in the booming economy of the twenties by some Chicago investors. Unfortunately for the investors, it was built functionally and without style. It consisted of three double-story wings of identical dormitory rooms that joined at a central hub that served as the lobby and dining hall. The rooms were without private baths, and the dining hall was without windows; neither the hotel nor the rural area attracted the free spenders of the twenties. The depression sealed its doom, and the investors vanished. The county eventually took over its operation, and the hotel has served variously as a site for a senior citizen center, classes on water safety, the Moose Lodge, and a bingo hall. By the early fifties the county found the hotel's maintenance too extravagant to justify its continued use, and it was offered for sale by closed bid.

Nathan Griswold, who had just retired from farming, made the only bid. Rumor had it that he only bid one dollar, but that could not have been possible since the county charter bound its board to sell public land at a reasonable market value. Nonetheless, the hotel became Nathan's and part of his plan for his "lakeside mansion." He owned the hotel for his remaining thirty-seven years and made the single improvement of boarding the doors and windows. Despite urging and outright threats from several county and town officials, Nathan steadfastly refused to sell or make any alterations to his property, and the hotel gradually deteriorated and its surrounding grounds returned to nature.

In my memory the hotel was always abandoned, sealed, and anonymous. I was about five when I first saw it. My father had taken me fishing in a boat for the first time, and I was more interested in riding in the boat than fishing. After what I am certain was constant begging, my father pulled in his lines and we rode around the lake. At its north end we made a sharp turn which delighted me, and I let go of the seat and slipped. When I climbed up I saw the hotel peering at me with its boarded windows that I thought were eyes of misery. As we headed to the dock, I did not take my eyes off those windows. In the car I asked my father about the hotel and its sad eyes. He explained in five-year-old logic that it was an old building, and it was sad because it didn't have any friends left. After that, I always thought of the hotel as a lonely place, and it made me feel the same.

Nathan died this past spring in the county nursing home, of natural causes, specifically, kidney failure, and since he left no heirs, the county reclaimed the hotel as partial compensation for his nursing home bill. Its demolition was approved at the next board meeting.

***

I found the road leading to the hotel with ease, largely because the heavy demolition equipment had flattened most of the weeds and saplings that had overgrown the original road. I had traveled about half its quarter-mile length when the hotel became visible through the trees. I saw the windows peering at me, and I felt a little lonely.

I parked in front of the hotel next to Bird's patrol car, a crane with a wrecking ball, and a partially-filled earth hauler. I had finished Emma's sandwich, and I fished my cigar out of the ashtray. I worked the end around in my mouth until it felt comfortable. I seldom lit my cigars, and one might last me several days before it disintegrated. I've tried to quit smoking for fifteen years; this is as close as I've come to success.

I saw Bird sitting on the steps that led to the lobby. He stretched his long legs and walked rapidly toward me. The demolition crew was gone, but they had knocked down the outside wall of one of the wings facing the lake. The exposed inner walls of the small rooms looked like a large honeycomb. By the time I had lifted my kit from the van, Bird was at my shoulder.

"Good, you brought it," he said.

"Yeah, you said to. Now, what's going on?"

"You just won't believe it. I got to show it to you. There's just no way to describe it. Come on."

Bird took off in the direction of the lobby. His long, rapid strides ate up the distance, and I had to trot to catch up.

"Hold up a minute, Bird. This kit is heavy. What's the rush?"

He stopped and gave me a puzzled look. "I don't know. They're not going anywhere."

"They?" I asked.

"Come on, you'll see," he said, and led me to a ladder that extended to the second story room nearest the lobby. He folded his legs and arms around the rungs and climbed to the top.

I am afraid of heights and had trepidations about climbing a ladder with my kit. "Christ, Bird. That the only way up?"

"Yeah. Come as far as you can, and I'll help you with the kit."

I put on my coveralls and pushed my kit up the ladder. Even with Bird's help, I was drenched with sweat by the time I pulled myself into the room. I blinked a few times to adjust to the dimmer light, and I saw them.

"Jesus Lord, Bird. What the hell is going on?"

Bird was wiping his face with his handkerchief. "I don't know. I told you I couldn't describe it. Those demo fellows were bumping this wall down just as nice as pie, and these things popped up. They called me right off, and I called you."

On the single bed lay two skeletons. At one time they had been bodies, but decomposition left only darkened bones with scant remnants of clothing and hair clinging to them. One was prone, and the second was positioned so that its breast bone met the first's spine and its legs straddled the first's thighs. The second's spine had been severed at the fifth vertebra, and those five poked out of its pelvis like a tree stump. Except for the stained bed on which they rested and a threadbare carpet full of plaster dust, the room was empty.

As a doctor I had seen my share of the unsavory in both life and death, but I had never seen anything like the dark bones on the bed. I looked at Bird quizzically.

He read my mental question. "God, Bill, I don't know. You're the ME. I thought you'd know what to do."

My duty as the medical examiner was to supply identity

and cause of death for any corpse and to perform any tests requested. This had always been obvious work before; now I was unsure where to start.

"I guess we'd better take some pictures first off," I said and bent to get my camera out of the kit. "We'll have to move them, and we should record the scene."

Bird's face relaxed. "I figured you'd know what to do."

I took a lot of pictures, partly to record the scene accurately, but mostly because, despite Bird's confidence, I wasn't certain what to do, and I needed time to collect my thoughts. I hadn't dealt with skeletons on a professional level; my last experience with one was in medical school. The names and locations of the bones and how to set them if they broke was the extent of my expertise. I did have some knowledge of forensics because a good deal of my surgical repair work was the result of crimes, but that knowledge had to do with body tissues and, generally, the entry and exit wounds of bullets from that tissue.

By the time I photographed every inch of the room, I knew the skeletons had to be examined by an outside specialist, probably a forensic anthropologist. My job, as I perceived it, was to preserve the bones and any other remnants so that those examinations could take place. I communicated this to Bird.

"Okay, I agree. But how are we going to do that?"

"We'll put them in body bags, and lay them out on my morgue tables," I said.

"Is it all right to move them?"

"Sure. No one could study them here. We have pictures of their positions, if that happens to be important, and mainly we just have to be careful not to mix the bones between the two. The anthropologist will go through them bone by bone and can probably tell us their sex, age, and race. I doubt if he could tell much else."

"What about dental records?" asked Bird. "Couldn't those identify them?"

"Sure, those would be great if you had some idea who the victims were. Then you could compare the records to the teeth and hope for a match. But we don't have any idea who those skeletons once belonged to, which would mean we would have to search every dental record in the country. Kind of impossible."

"Yeah, I guess," Bird said. He pushed some plaster chips with his toe. "I guess I'm used to more tangible stuff."

"So am I, Bird, so am I. Let's go down and get the bags." I pointed to the door to the hall. "Any reason we can't use the stairs like civilized people? I hate going down ladders."

"Guess so, if they aren't knocked down or something," Bird said, and pulled on the door. "Damned thing's stuck. Looks like the ladder after all."

"Jesus, Bird. It really scares me."

"Okay, you big pussy. I'll go get the bags and shove the door open from the outside. Then you won't have to use the big bad ladder." Bird clearly found humor in my acrophobia and chuckled as he descended.

"Go screw yourself," I said. I removed the cigar from my mouth and examined the pulverized end. I tossed it out the open wall. "Bring me a cigar from the glove compartment, will you, Bird?"

"You smoke too much," he called over his shoulder. His long stride had taken him halfway to the van.

"Haven't seen me smoke yet," I shouted after him.

I stood a few feet from the open wall to accommodate my

fear and looked at the lake. The summer sun was well above the horizon, but it cast shadows of the trees on the water. The air was oppressively still, and in front of the hotel the glassy surface of the water was broken only by the small wake of a family of ducks. I could hear the throb of the ski boat motors coming from the middle of the lake as tourists made use of the hot weather and long days.

I saw Bird enter the lobby, and I crossed to the door to give him assistance. A moment or two later I heard Bird call me through the door.

"Bill, can you hear me?"

"Yeah, want me to pull?"

"Bill, you got to come around here."

"What? Jesus, Bird, can't you open the door?"

"No, I can't. And you have to come around here."

CHAPTER TWO

Bird's voice had taken on a calm quality that he used in stressful situations. Reluctantly, I approached the ladder. I had just seen Bird throw his legs over the side of the ladder and step down its rungs like he was going down my porch steps. My attempt was less graceful and involved grasping the remains of the carpet with one hand for several moments until I convinced myself that the ladder would hold me. My descent progressed with single steps and several halts to wait out any jiggling movements. I was soaked with sweat when I made it to the bottom. "This better be important," I said to myself as I crossed to the lobby and made my way up the stairs.

I saw Bird standing in the hall, staring at the wall. "Well, what the hell is so damned important?" I asked.

"This," he said and pointed to the wall.

I looked. It was a wall. "I don't get it."

"Go open the first door," Bird said, not taking his eyes off the wall.

I did and was surprised to find it opened easily. I was more surprised to find the skeletons missing. I looked at Bird, who was still staring at the wall. "What's going on?" I asked.

"See how much space there is between the beginning of the hall and the first door?" Bird asked.

I was getting annoyed with his game, but I looked. I looked at the rest of the hall and its uniformly placed doors. "Yeah, it's a lot of space, but ... Oh. That first door was walled up."

"You got it," said Bird, and ran his fingers over the wall. "Good job, too. Nice and smooth, no cracks. Matching paint. Impossible to notice unless you were looking for it."

I took the cigar that Bird had stored in his shirt pocket. I unwrapped it and got it comfortable in my mouth. "Bird, I think we can rule out accidental death for these two," I said.

We looked at the wall silently for a minute. I heard Bird sigh. In a voice forced calm, he explained that he would retrieve my camera for me so that I would not have to climb the ladder again. He said he would get his crowbar from his trunk and tear out the wall covering the door. He wanted pictures of the wall and pictures as he tore it down. He explained this all in unnecessary detail that I recognized as one of the coping techniques he used when he was confused or nervous. I started to follow him, but stopped myself. Bird would think it through and adjust.

When Bird returned with the camera and crowbar, he had regained his composure, and explained how he wanted the wall photographed. I made the adjustments to the camera, and Bird tapped the wall with this crowbar. "Don't sound like much of a hollow place," he said. "But I think the door should be about here. Did you get all those pictures?"

"I need you to get out of the way first," I said. "Unless you want to be in them."

"Uh, no," Bird said, and stepped out of the way. "Be sure to get the blank wall and the hallway that shows the empty space."

"I will," I said and snapped off some pictures.

Bird slammed the end of the crowbar into the wall, and a cloud of dust puffed and settled to the floor. "I'll be damned," he said. "That's plaster and lath. No wonder it sounded solid. Get a picture of this, too."

I dutifully snapped a picture of the hole that revealed pieces of lathing. "Get some of that plaster off so I can get a better shot."

"I'm going to," Bird said, and used the crowbar like a hammer to break the plaster.

A half hour later the floor was filled with plaster chunks, the air was white with dust, and the doorway was visible. Its molding had been removed to make a flush surface for the plaster; the lathing had been nailed directly across the frame.

"That was really a good job of plastering," Bird said as he wiped sweat and dust from his face. The dust had turned his dark hair white, and had collected in the creases of his uniform. I supposed that I was in a similar condition.

"I'm going to pull this lathing down," he said. "Did you get pictures?"

"Yeah, several."

After the lathing was removed, the door opened easily by the knob, and we were again faced with the skeletons. Bird wiped his face again and smeared milky sweat under his chin. "That was a job. What now?"

I pulled on a pair of surgical gloves. "Now it's my turn to work."

"Need me to help?" Bird asked.

"Best if you don't. I want to have as little trace on the bones as possible. As it is they're full of plaster dust, but there wasn't much we could do about that. I'm going to bag them and take samples of the materials in the room for elimination purposes on the outside chance there might be some significant material on the bones. Guess you can take it easy for a while."

"Good. I worked up quite a sweat. Still hot out," Bird said, and he sat on the floor and hung his legs out the open wall. Looking at him that close to the edge gave me a chill, and I looked at the solid floor and prepared the bag. Bird turned to watch me place the bones in the bag.

"Why are they all loose?" he asked.

"No tissue left to hold them together. Those skeletons you saw in school were wired together. Actually, we're lucky the skeletons were in this room where nothing could disturb them. If they'd been outside, wind and water and animals would've moved the bones all over. Probably never would've found all of them."

"Won't they get mixed up in the bag?"

"Yeah, but they'll all be laid out on a table for the forensic anthropologist to study. I think I remember the proper order, and I'm sure he does."

"Forensic anthropologist?"

"Yeah, the specialist I told you I was going the call for help."

I put the first skull in the bag last, tried to gather as much of its black, curly hair as possible, and zipped the bag shut. Crude as it might be, the bag was the first decent treatment for whoever this was who'd ended his life sealed in a hotel room. I examined the bones of the second skeleton to be certain that I hadn't missed any from the first, and I placed its bones in the second bag. Some of its bones were encrusted with a dried mildew type substance that stuck them to the bed sheets. I supposed that this represented the last of the decomposition; a few simple cells sucking nutrients from what had once been a life.

I pulled the pelvis free from the dried slime, and I saw a piece of metal. I grabbed it with a pair of tweezers, and held it up to the light.

"Bird, I think this could help establish the cause of death for one of these."

Bird turned from his view of the lake. "Why, that's a bullet. Where'd it come from?"

"From that slime on the bed. Small caliber, probably a twenty-two pistol. I'd say one of them was shot, the bullet remained in his body, and fell out when the tissue decomposed."

"Anything else in that stuff?" Bird asked, and I probed with tweezers and produced some buttons.

"Looks like all of it," I said. "The bullet is the only significant item."

Bird shoved his fingers through his hair, raising a puff of plaster dust. "Yeah. Guess there really was a murder here. But how long ago?"

"I can't say for sure. The anthropologist should be able to date them pretty accurately, but I'd guess they've been here a long time. Decomposition is complete, there's no moisture, and no one has been in here for years and years."

"I don't think anyone's been in the hotel itself for years. I'll bet Nathan came and went as he pleased."

I looked at Bird. "You think Nathan had something to do with this?"

"Well, who else? He owned the place. I don't know of anyone else who's been in here since he bought it."

"Bird, Nathan's dead and he was old. He wasn't walking very well when I left for California."

"But he owned the hotel a long time before you ever thought of California." Bird threw his arms out to emphasize his point. He looked like a water crane taking off. I suppressed a smile. Actually, Bird did have a point: Nathan had owned the hotel for almost four decades, more than enough time for a body to decompose. "You could be right, Bird," I said. "I hope it's that simple."

"Yeah, me too. You finished?"

"Just got to get some material samples and drop this bullet in an evidence bag and that should do it."

***

After we had loaded the two bags into the van, Bird and I leaned on the front fender of his patrol car and watched the lake darken as the sun set. He tried to clean some of the dust off his pants, but succeeded mostly in smearing it.

"Quite a day," I said. "I just get home and find out that Maria called and then this."

"Maria?" Bird snapped his head upright, the plaster forgotten. "What did that bitch want?"

"Hey, man, she's my ex-wife, not yours. And I don't know. I haven't called her back yet."

"Don't. Serve the bitch right."

"You're in a foul mood, Bird," I said. "Excuse the pun."

Bird didn't smile. "Yeah, I am. I was planning on a little fishing this week, but I expect that's out of the question what with the stir those are going to cause." He nodded to my van. "Besides, I don't like Maria."

"Why? You weren't married to her."

"Yeah, but I watched her take my best buddy, who, in high school showed enough smarts and personality to be running a hospital or a company or the government or something, and she turned him into you. And now you hide from people in books and emergency rooms and in dead bodies. You think I don't know why you wanted to be the ME? Dead people don't talk, that's why. You have longer conversations with your car than you do with people. She made you scared of any type of relationship with people. That's why I don't like her."

"I'm not exactly scared," I said defensively. "I just don't have a lot of friends."

"My point exactly," he said. "In any case, you could have really been somebody, done something. Not this middle-aged guy who drinks too much, fiddles with an old car, and tries to figure out why some ninety-year-old woman died. She took all the life out of you."

I bit my tongue to stop my angry torrent. I was miserable at thinking on my feet; in verbal confrontations I either lost due to my silence or lost due to my vitriolic response. Bird was my best and probably only friend; I didn't want to offend him, but I didn't want him to assail my life either. I chewed my cigar vigorously and looked at the lake.

Bird was equally uncomfortable. He kicked at a dandelion with his boot, blew his nose, and rummaged in his pockets. "Hey, I'm sorry I blew off like that. Your life is your business. I guess all this has me edgy. I usually don't even see dead *bodies,* let alone skeletons. We just don't have that kind of excitement in Bishop. Hell, you know that. I hate to think of what will happen when this gets out. Rumors, newspapers, television, and all of it coming at me."

"Think so?" I asked.

"Shit, those demo fellows are down at the Golden Eagle right now drinking beer and telling the best story of their lives. Before I get home every town leader and crackpot will have called me. Won't be any rest until we get some answers. And Ervin Johnston will get his needle nose in it."

Ervin Johnston ran the local paper and was Bird's nemesis; he was notorious for manufacturing scandals and misrepresenting facts. No one took him very seriously, but Bird would be deluged with questions. Suddenly, I realized that neither of us could answer the most basic question.

"Bird," I said, "there's two more wings of rooms."

"Yeah, so?" he responded, then shoved himself off the fender and stood bolt upright. "How could I be so stupid? Christ, a rookie would have checked the other rooms. Been here half a damn afternoon, and I never even thought of it. Shit."

"Put it off to shock. This doesn't happen everyday," I said.

Bird was retrieving the flashlights from his trunk. "Maybe so. But don't tell anyone how stupid I was. Come on." He pushed a flashlight at me and strode off to the hotel.

The second wing also faced the lake, but it extended westward from the lobby. The door to the first room on the second floor had been sealed; the same condition existed in the third wing that extended rearward from the lobby. We found the sealed doors directly, but we spent another hour shining circles of light into every room and onto every wall. When Bird was satisfied that no other anomalies existed, we returned to the lobby.

Bird wiped the sweat from his eyes with the back of his hand. "Well, likely there's something in those other two rooms, and I guess we'd better find out what."

I had shed my coveralls before we began the search, but I was still dripping with sweat. "Tonight? Christ, Bird, it's hot as hell and it's dark."

"Be hotter tomorrow. I'm going to call Jim to get the emergency lights."

I didn't say anything and he continued, "Look, I know it's a bitch, but if we wait until tomorrow, every tourist, reporter, and kid from here to Chicago will be sitting on top of us. You want to work like that?"

Reluctantly, I admitted he was right, but suggested that we try to look in the outside windows first to see if there was anything to deal with. Bird agreed, and we shone our lights on the second story windows. We saw solid brick where the windows should have been.

"Damn," I said, "did they brick the windows, too?"

"I don't think so," said Bird. "Those bricks look as weathered as the others and the laying pattern seems unbroken. I don't think any of those first rooms had windows."

"What? Why not?"

"Construction, probably. This hotel was built a long time ago and, from what I understand, in a hurry. I bet they needed a solid wall near the hub to take the stress from the roof. The first room probably didn't have a window either, but we couldn't tell because the wall was knocked down."

"Be damned," I said. "Whoever did this picked the perfect place: a sealed, windowless room. Sounds like Edgar Allen Poe."

"Yeah. Just created a burial vault is what happened. Made a grave," said Bird.

CHAPTER THREE

We stared at the wall for a couple of minutes. "Well," Bird said, "I'm going to have Mary raise Jim to get those lights. I think I'll call my wife and have her bring me something to eat. You want anything?"

I was still full from Emma's sandwich, but I was dying of thirst. "Ice water, lots of it. And brandy," I added.

I could see Bird scowl in the darkness. "Water, yes. Brandy, no," he said. "You're on duty."

"Under kind of unusual circumstances," I argued. "It's going to be a long night. I need something to keep me going."

"My ass would be grass if anyone found out."

"So who's going to tell?" I asked, immaturely.

"Jesus Christ," Bird spat out. "I'm not having this conversation. If you don't know enough not to drink on duty by now, and if you think you can keep secrets in this town, then I can't help you anymore. Drink yourself to death like you were when you came back."

"Calm down, Bird. If it bothers you, forget I said anything. And I don't drink much anymore. I just sip some brandy in the evening. I haven't been drunk in years. Since there aren't any secrets in this town, you should know that," I said.

"Well, yeah, I guess," he admitted. "But you're not drinking anything but water and soda pop when you're on duty. That sort of thing get out, and they'll be looking hard at both of us."

"Okay, Bird. No sweat. Tell your wife to bring me some ice water." I tried not to show my annoyance to Bird, but I resented his protection. While it was true that I hit the booze pretty heavily after my father died, I controlled it now, and I didn't think Bird should be telling me my business. He was right about the lack of secrets in a small town, though. I was used to the anonymity in Los Angeles where resumes and credit ratings are more real than people. I had heard rumors to the effect that Bird did me a favor by making me the ME, despite the fact that I was more than qualified and no one else wanted it. Rumors had a way of becoming the truth, and, consequently, any of my failures would tarnish Bird.

When Bird returned from talking to his wife and deputy, we sat on the steps that led to the lobby and waited. Neither of us mentioned the brandy again.

Bird pointed to a rough patch of concrete at the bottom of the steps. "Used to be a lion right there, sitting on a kind of pedestal. Sort of divided the stairs in half."

"How do you know that?"

"Used to play on it when I was maybe three."

"What were you doing out here?" I asked.

"This was a senior center for awhile. Used some of the rooms as a kind of nursing home. My granddad was here, and when we'd visit my mom would bring me out here to play on the lion. I guess granddad died in there. Anyway, we stopped coming."

"That must have been just before Nathan bought it and boarded it up," I said.

Bird calculated a moment. "Yeah, that's right. Maybe that's why we stopped coming and granddad died later. I can't really remember. I was only about three. But I remember climbing on that lion. I thought it was huge." Bird laughed, "Probably wasn't two feet high."

We heard a car motor straining on the rough road, and a moment later we saw headlights dance in the trees.

"I suspect that's Jim," Bird said. "I hope he brought everything." He strode off to meet his deputy, and I followed, not trying to match Bird's pace.

When I reached Jim's patrol car, Bird shoved a Thermos of water at me, and opened a soda. We both drank copiously, and trickles of water ran down my chin and dampened my shirt. Bird poked in a cooler and produced a container of his wife's fried chicken and another of potato salad. He offered them to me, and I accepted a leg, Bird inhaled a breast, a thigh, and most of the potato salad. He opened another soda and belched noisily, "Guess I was hungry," he said, and wiped his hands and face with the wet rag that his wife had thoughtfully packed.

"I guess so," I said. "Good chicken." I pitched the leg bone over my shoulder. "More for later?"

Bird extracted a second container of chicken from the cooler. "My wife knows me well," he said. "Well, I guess we'd better get to work."

The three of us lugged the lights and the generator to the lobby. Bird set the generator by the door to vent the exhaust and ran the extension cord to the second wing. Jim and I followed with the lights, crowbars, and a sledge hammer. Bird directed the lights on the sealed door and asked Jim what he had heard about this in town.

"Nothing that makes much sense," he said. "Something about bodies buried in the walls and a sacrificial altar in the basement."

"Just takes a minute for stories to start," Bird sucked at some chicken caught in his teeth. "To put it right for you, the demo fellows did find two bodies that had been reduced to skeletons. Bill and I later determined that the room they were in had been sealed. We've looked the place over good and there's no altar or any crap like that, but we found two more sealed rooms. I expect we'll find something in them, too."

"Jesus," said Jim, "sounds like *The Twilight Zone*."

"Yes, it does," said Bird. "Yes, it does." He was running his fingers over the wall and glanced at me. "Got the camera, Bill?"

"Yeah, step back, and I'll get the first shot."

Bird and Jim knocked the plaster from the doorway and removed the lathing while I took pictures. The door again opened easily by the knob.

"Well, I guess we got to look," said Bird. "Jim, pull those lights in here."

The windowless room contained a threadbare carpet, a three-drawer dresser, and a single bed with two more skeletons. When the lights hit them Jim flinched backwards. "God Almighty," he said. "This like the other room? How on earth ..?"

"Pretty much like the other one," Bird cut him off. He was standing with his arms folded, staring at the skeletons with an air of resignation, as if he had just had bad news confirmed.

These skeletons were in the same condition as the first pair. A few scraps of fabric clung to the darkened bones, patches of hair clung to the skulls and bed sheet. The sheet itself was stained with a black residue. The positions of the skeletons were different from the first pair. One lay supine, with its skull pressed into the bed. The second skeleton's breast bone rested on the first's, and its frontal skull was likewise buried in the bed. Their pelvises met, and the two sets of legs covered the remainder of the bed. I pulled on my coveralls, sent Jim for my kit, and began taking pictures. Bird drifted out of the room, muttering that he'd probably never fish again.

It took me about an hour to separate and bag the bones, get material samples, and poke through the crusted slime on the sheets. I found some more buttons, but no bullets or anything else that would serve as a murder weapon. The cause of death for this pair would likely be undetermined. We loaded the bags into the van and lugged the equipment to the third sealed doorway.

After I snapped some pictures, Bird smashed the crowbar through the wall and said, "I wonder what we'll find in here." He took a couple of half swings with the sledge hammer and turned it over to Jim. He stood beside me as I snapped pictures as the doorway was revealed. "If they had torn this damn building down years ago like they should have, we wouldn't be standing here now," he said.

"I think that's pretty obvious, Bird," I said.

"You know damned good and well what I mean," he shot back. No building, no place for Nathan to make his torture chambers, and no murders for me to deal with."

"I know, Bird, but I'll help you."

He rolled his eyes in mock horror, "Now I know I'm doomed." He grinned for a minute. "But I sure didn't want nothing like this in my life."

Jim cleared the door, and we pulled in the lights. The room appeared identical to the first two: threadbare carpet, small dresser, and a single bed with two skeletons. When the light steadied, I saw I was wrong. In my medical career I had seen fetuses in all types of conditions. I had even delivered one that had been shot and operated on it to remove the bullet from its lung. It lived. But I had never seen the skeleton of a fetus within the skeleton of its mother, which was what lay on the bed. I involuntarily stepped back and into Bird. "Jesus, Mary, and Joseph," I stammered.

Bird caught my reaction. "What is it … Good Christ. How could that happen?"

"Mother died, baby died," I said through clenched teeth. "Shit, man, I don't like this."

Jim took a surreptitious look. "Is that real?" he whispered.

I assured him it was, and he left the room for several minutes. He looked a little pale when he returned, and I assumed he had been sick. The three of us stared at the remains of a life for whom the womb had become a grave.

"This just gets weirder and weirder." Bird broke the silence and flapped his arms against his sides. "I can't get any sense to this at all. Who'd kill a pregnant woman?"

I had seen several killed in the violence of south central Los Angeles, but most had been hit by stray bullets. I couldn't think of any that had been killed purposely.

"You were pretty sure Nathan was responsible," I reminded him.

"I'm not sure I'm on planet Earth anymore," Bird muttered and sighed. "What do you want us to do?"

I snapped on a pair of fresh gloves. "Nothing. Just keep the generator going. I'll be about an hour."

Jim beat Bird to the door, and I heard him pick his way down the stairs to the lobby.

"Guess I better check on him," Bird said, as he followed. "Holler if you need anything."

I waved my hand in assent and began the tasks that by now had become routine. I began with pictures, and then separated the bones into body bags. The mother was supine, and the bones of her fetus lay clustered around her spine and pelvis. Because the fetus' bones were fine and soft, actually little more than cartilage, I wrapped them carefully in gauze before I transferred them into the bag.

The sixth skeleton was partially off the bed. The upper torso lay prone between the mother's legs with its skull nearly resting on the mother's pelvis. Its own pelvis and legs rested on the floor. I guessed that it had been kneeling over the bed and wondered if its owner had been trying to deliver the baby. Birth is a dangerous act, which could explain the deaths of the mother and fetus, but didn't explain the death of the second person and certainly not the sealed door. Bird was right. It was just plain weird.

When I was collecting the material samples I noticed something under the dresser. I pulled it out and saw a small lattice in the shape of a trapezoid. Strangely, it was made entirely of woven sticks; no nails, staples, or glue was apparent. I could fathom no use for it, and assumed it was left by some long-ago guest. Without really knowing why, I dropped it into an evidence bag.

I found Bird and Jim sitting on the outside steps where Bird had played on the lion two generations ago. I threw my cigar past them into the weeds. "Let's load up," I said.

By the time we finished it was almost two in the morning.

Bird sent Jim down the lane first, and Bird and I stayed behind to wrap crime scene tape around the lobby doors and as much of the exposed wing as possible.

"Think this will do any good?" I asked.

"No, I'm just following procedure. I already told Jim to get back here at dawn to fend off the curious." Bird stretched his arms and arched his back. "Shit, I'm beat. What do you think, Bill?"

"I think I'm beat, too," I said.

"No, about this. What do you think happened?"

"Six people and an unborn baby died a long time ago. One was probably shot. I don't think we're going to know much more than that. That hotel held its secret a long time. I don't think it's going to give it up very easy."

"Probably not," said Bird. "Let's go home and get some rest. Be all hell tomorrow."

***

It was after three when I parked the van in my driveway. Except for the street lights and an occasional porch light, Bishop was dark and deserted. In Los Angeles, traffic jams occurred at three in the morning, and main streets were never without activity; in Bishop most people believed that little worthwhile took place after dark.

In fact, there was very little about which the people of Bishop disagreed. Men, and many women, worked daily, families went to church on Sundays, parents turned out for Back to School nights and Christmas festivals. Neighbors knew and trusted each other, and I knew that at this moment the majority of the doors were unlocked.

I had pondered from time to time the reasons for the vast

differences in lifestyles between Bishop and Los Angeles, and perhaps any small town and any metropolis. I had no definite conclusion, but thought it might reflect the fact that everyone in Bishop had descended from the same Northern European stock. Bishop had no minorities or recent immigrants, and nothing to attract them. The result was a town of one culture, with people of similar behavior types and expectations. Los Angeles had hundreds of nationalities and cultures. Each group practiced a different set of customs and held different beliefs. In such a situation conflicts became inevitable.

I left the bags in the van, figuring that tomorrow would be soon enough to lay them out in the morgue. I trudged through my door, discarded my coveralls, washed, and poured myself a generous portion of brandy. "Bird, be damned," I thought as the first swallow spread relaxing warmth through my body. I settled into my chair and propped my feet on the coffee table. After the second swallow, I fell asleep.

CHAPTER FOUR

Sometime in the night I found my way to my bed. Bright sunlight through a window whose shade I'd neglected to pull awakened me. My watch showed nine thirty, and I silently congratulated myself for nearly six hours of continuous sleep. Because of my years of irregular hours, I had become accustomed to surviving on naps, and I rarely slept through the night. Despite feeling rested, I had a nagging discomfort in the back of my mind. I recognized this as a precursor to something unpleasant. The feeling persisted while I showered, and I mentally relived the events of the previous night to determine its cause. By the time I was dressed, I was no closer to the solution, but I was certain that it was not caused by either the skeletons or the hotel.

I saw the cause of my discomfiture in the living room: the blinking light of my message machine. I hadn't called my ex-wife.

"Damn you to hell," I said to the machine and wondered if I should call her now and fume about it during breakfast, or call later and worry about it during breakfast. Either way, breakfast was ruined.

Despite living alone for twenty years, my culinary talents extended only to breakfast, and actually only to bacon and eggs. I had made several attempts at pancakes through the years, but never seemed to be able to make any without raw batter inside. I retrieved my frying pan from the oven, lit a burner and tossed in six strips of bacon. As they began to sizzle, I beat three eggs and put some bread in the toaster. I turned the bacon and poured my juice. By then the bacon was cooked, and I placed the strips on a paper towel to drain. I poured some of the grease out of the pan and dumped in the eggs. While they cooked, I buttered my toast. If I followed that routine precisely, I never undercooked or burned anything. I tried to develop a similar routine for dinner, but it had too many variables. I usually ate out.

After breakfast I dialed my ex-wife's number and listened to the rings, hoping she would be gone. She wasn't.

"Hello," she said. Her voice was always pleasant at first, and I remembered her soft hazel eyes that enchanted me years ago.

"Hi, Maria," I said. "It's me. How're things?"

"Well, it's about time you called. You out all night with some bitch?" Her tone lost any hint of pleasantness, or even civility, and I knew I was in for a bad time.

"No, I was working. Kind of an interesting case. You might hear about it on the news—"

"I don't care about that or your silly job. You've got a problem."

Experience told me that meant she had a problem that she expected me to fix. "Oh, what's my problem?" I asked wearily.

"Don't get smart with me," she snapped back. "It's your son," she added.

I shifted to the edge of the chair. "What about Paul? Is he hurt?"

"No, nothing like that," she said languidly, knowing that she had me hooked. "He lost the money you sent him for his tuition."

I settled back in the chair half-relieved that my son was all right and half-upset about the money. "You mean he lost the check?" I asked.

"No, he cashed the check and lost the money. Actually, he didn't lose it. He bought a car."

"A car?"

"Actually, he just made the down payment on it. It's a BMW."

"What?" I was incredulous. "He bought a BMW?" BMWs represented yuppies to me, and I tried very hard not to emulate their lifestyles. I also knew that even the 300 series BMW was beyond my means and certainly beyond Paul's.

"That's what I said, a BMW. It's dark green. Nice car," said Maria.

"It should be for the price."

"He got an excellent deal, and he looks so good in the car. Just like a real businessman."

A real businessman with no business and no money, I thought, but kept the thought silent and said, "I'm sure he does. But how is he going to pay his tuition?"

"That's what I called about. Oh, hold on a second."

I shifted my weight in the chair and concluded that the next news I'd hear was that Paul was dropping out of college. Although I wasn't pleased with the news, I had anticipated it for some time. College required intelligence and discipline, and Paul had the former, but not the latter. His mother, I was sure, didn't provide much support or guidelines for such mundane things as studying and research. She was more pleased that he looked good in a car. I was surprised that he had made it through his junior year.

"Okay, I'm back," I heard in the receiver. "The cat was pulling tissue out of the trash. Honestly, it just goes on and on."

"Yeah, I know what you mean," I mumbled, my mind on Paul.

"No, you don't," she retorted. "You just live by yourself. I had to do everything. I had to raise Paul; you weren't around. I had to give him a home and let him know somebody cared. It wasn't easy. I've given my life to that boy of yours."

I had heard this tirade before, and I bit my lip until it hurt. I wanted to remind her that it was she who divorced me and left the state. She who forgot to give me her current phone numbers; she who sent Paul to camp during my visitation periods; she who failed to deliver my messages and mail to Paul, and said God knows what to him about me. But she would play a martyr for raising that boy of mine. I wanted to say all that, but instead I said, "I'm sure it wasn't."

"Well, it hasn't been," said Maria, somewhat mollified. "Anyway, Paul needs another check."

This caught me off guard. I was expecting an announcement about his termination of college, not a request for more money. "What for?" I asked.

"For the tuition, Dummy. He has to have it paid by the first of August."

She was right; I *was* dumb. I hadn't seen a plea for money coming anywhere in the conversation. "Maria," I said, "that check was for sixty-five hundred dollars. That was all the money I had."

"Paul needs to go to college," she said forcefully. "And you can't expect me to pay for it. After all, I take care of everything else."

I vaguely wondered what "everything else" involved, and said, "Be that as it may, I don't have any more money."

"Well, just what is he supposed to do?" Maria was getting angry; her pitch had risen and she was emphasizing pronouns.

"He could sell his car or get a job," I said, and knew I had thrown fuel on her anger.

"That's not fair. He needs college. You got yours, and I helped you get it. Now you're denying your own son. Some father you turned out to be."

I bit my lip again. I had attended college and medical school for twelve years, and the extent of Maria's help consisted of typing my English papers when I was a sophomore. "I'm not denying him. I gave him the money, and he bought a car. I don't have any more money." I heard a pleading tone in my voice, and I made a conscious effort to remove it.

"If you were a real doctor, you'd have money. But no, you want to fiddle with poor people and old people who could care less about you," Maria taunted.

"Well, that's my job," I said evenly.

Maria paused; since I didn't rise to her taunt, she lost her place. My respite didn't last long.

"I'm sending Paul to see you this week. You get it all straight and him into college. Honestly, I don't know why I thought you'd understand this. You're as dense as you ever were," Maria declared and slammed her receiver to announce the end of the conversation.

I said goodbye to the dial tone and sank back into my chair. The call had exhausted me, as most conversations with

Maria did. I wanted to go back to bed, but was too enervated to get out of the chair. While I waited for my energy level to stabilize, I calculated my assets to determine if I could again finance Paul's tuition. Short of taking another mortgage, I saw no possible way. Besides, I told myself, he was a man, and he'd made a choice. I figured that I couldn't do anything about the situation until I talked to Paul, and I should stop worrying about it. I needed something to occupy my mind, and the skeletons provided it. I felt some energy return, and as I looked for my keys, I was planning my procedures for their examinations.

CHAPTER FIVE

In Bishop, the medical examiner's office and morgue occupied a section of the pathology lab in the county hospital.
My office was a cubby hole with room for a desk and a file
cabinet; the morgue consisted of a wall of refrigerated drawers
and an autopsy table. I was granted, however, full use of the
pathology lab, not that I'd ever needed it. Today, I borrowed six
of their tables and wheeled them into the morgue. I unloaded
the bags of skeletons from the van and placed one on each
table; I put the fetus on the autopsy table. I donned my lab
coat, stuck a fresh cigar in my mouth, and went to work.

In my first year of medical school, I learned all the bones
in the human body. I could name them, locate them, and
identify them. But that was a long time ago, and I rarely had
any need for that knowledge in my practice of medicine. As I
arranged the bones from the first bag, I was pleased that the
knowledge returned. I laid the bones so that they would be
conducive to examination: the ribs were placed on opposite
sides of the spine, the arms outside the ribs, and with space
between all major joints. I wrapped the skull in gauze to pre-

serve its remaining hair, and checked my work with a reference book. Outside of misplacing the first and second finger bones, I had a properly arranged skeleton. I silently congratulated myself, and examined the bones closely.

Aside from their dark color, which could be normal for all I knew, the only abnormality was a chip on the third rib. I guessed that the bullet had glanced off this rib before embedding itself in flesh and organs. Beyond that, I was unable to make any further conclusions. I knew that a skeleton could yield much information about the person, but I had no experience in that area. I only wished to have them in good order for the anthropologist.

I repeated the procedure with the other skeletons, with the exception of the fetus, which I left wrapped in its protective gauze on the autopsy table. I examined each bone as I laid it out, but I was unable to discern any other information. I labeled each table by numbers, and as soon as I developed the film, each would be identified by its pictures from the hotel. Satisfied with my work, I locked the morgue door and went to eat a late lunch in the cafeteria.

I found a tuna sandwich and a couple of bananas that looked passable. Betty, the cashier, put down her book and punched numbers.

"Two fifty, Doc," she said. "How come you're here on Sunday, anyway?"

"Little work to catch up. How's school?"

"Okay, I guess. But summer school goes fast. No time to rest."

"You're young," I said. "You don't need rest. How much more you got?"

"If I get all my classes, I'll graduate next June. You coming to my graduation?"

"You bet. But you'll have to remind me."

"I will. Hey, Doc, you working on those bones from the hotel?"

"How do you know about that?"

"Oh, everybody knows," she said and tossed some hair out of her face. "The Des Moines news team interviewed Bird a couple of hours ago. So what's the deal, Doc?"

"Betty," I said with all seriousness, "you probably know more than I do."

I ate lunch and marveled at the speed of communication in a small town. Eighteen hours ago the only people who had known about the skeletons were myself, Bird, Jim, and a couple of demolition workers. Now, according to Betty, they were common knowledge. Los Angeles had faxes, twenty-four hour news stations, and cellular phones, and none of them could match small town gossip.

Bird had been right about the media. I suspected that once his interview was seen Bishop would have droves of visitors. Maybe that old hotel really would bring the tourists to Bishop after all.

My next task was to develop the pictures. I wasn't the official crime photographer, not that the county had one, but the sheriff's station had a developer of the same type that was used in one-hour photo places that I knew how to use. A wall of humidity met me as I left the hospital, and the interior of the van was like an uncontrolled sauna. "Typical Iowa afternoon," I muttered and punched the air conditioner button.

I was surprised to find Mary operating the switch board. The station was usually empty on Sundays, and the calls were routed to Bird's house. "Shit, Mary. Don't you ever go home?"

"It's been unbelievable," she said. "It started about noon,

hit its peak after Bird's interview, and just let up a few minutes ago."

"It?" I asked.

"The phone. I think everyone in the state called. I had to sort out the important ones and put them through to Bird. I'm beat." She put her head back and rubbed her eyes.

"Where's Bird?"

"Out at the hotel dealing with reporters, television crews, and people."

"Who called that was important?" I asked.

"Oh, our state representative. I can never remember his name, and I just said it an hour ago. Somebody from the state police, and reporters. I never knew so many newspapers and television stations existed. Couple of people called saying that the bones belonged to their long lost relatives."

"Well, kind of perks up an afternoon. I'm going to develop some pictures."

"Swell. Don't make a mess. I got enough to deal with," Mary said without opening her eyes.

I heard the phone ring as I walked down the hall, and I wondered how long I could avoid the media circus. My experiences with reporters in Los Angeles had given me a negative view of them. Their standard procedure seemed to be to shove a microphone in a family member's face and ask how it felt that his mother, father, sister, wife, child had just been killed. I was asked more than once how it felt when a patient died, and one reporter asked why I let the victim die and the criminal live. He broadcast my response, which was to try to flush his microphone down a toilet. It wouldn't flush, but it was ruined. I had to buy a replacement and was reprimanded by the hospital, but reporters shunned me, which made it a small price to pay.

I made double prints of each exposure, and identified them by skeleton number and hotel room number. I annotated the pictures of the rooms themselves, the hallways, and the sealed doorways on the reverse side. When I finished I had two sets of photos organized by skeleton and room. I considered leaving Bird's set in his office, but realized that with reporters around they might not be safe. I decided to store both sets in my kit until I heard from Bird.

Mary's switchboard was lit, and she was on the phone when I left. I tapped on the counter and waved. She raised her eyebrows in acknowledgment. On my way home I noticed that Emma's Deli was open, which was unusual for a Sunday. My thoughts returned to her special sandwich, brandy, and my novel. I figured I could still have a little enjoyment this weekend, and I turned and parked in front of her store.

"Hey, Emma. You open?" I called through the door.

Emma straightened and looked over the counter. She pushed a gray strand back into her hair net. "Yes and no. Bird asked me to get some sandwiches ready for Jim and some news people. You want something, too?"

"Sure would like one of your specials. Didn't really get to enjoy last night's."

"If you don't mind waiting a few minutes, I'll fix you up."

"No problem." I went to the cooler for a cold drink and held the can to my head to relieve the heat.

"I'm out of Muenster cheese," Emma said and plopped my sandwich on the counter. "I don't get my delivery until tomorrow, and I didn't expect to be open today."

"That's okay. Looks like this could be good for business," I said.

Emma replaced another strand of hair. "I had enough business. What I lack is peace. I'll put that on your tab."

As I pulled away and started a U-turn on Main Street, a sedan took my place in front of Emma's. I completed the turn and passed by as the driver opened the door with WHO emblazoned on it. Unfortunately, the driver, who was young, blond, and for some reason wearing a tie, also saw MEDICAL EXAMINER-BISHOP COUNTY on the side of my van. In my rear view mirror I saw him watch the van for several seconds before he turned into Emma's. I knew that my appointment with the media wouldn't be far off.

***

An hour later I was comfortably ensconced in my recliner with my feet propped on the coffee table, glass of brandy balanced on its arm and a cigar moistening in my mouth. I was on the last chapter of my mystery novel, and was thoroughly enjoying myself.

My doorbell startled me upright. Since no one visited me except Bird, who usually knocked, doorbells generally announced Jehovah's Witnesses and candy-selling kids. I took a swallow of brandy and made my way across the room, annoyed at being disturbed. I was surprised to find Paul standing on the porch.

"Hey, Paul," I said. "Come in. I wasn't expecting you this soon." I tried to remove any irritation from my voice and give an enthusiastic greeting. I doubted if I succeeded.

Paul caught the screen door that I pushed open and entered. To my additional surprise, he was followed by a girl in shorts and halter top. Once she was in the lighted room, I recognized her. She worked at the massage parlor in the amusement park at the south end of the lake. The parlor was Bishop's version of a whorehouse, which, I heard, did quite a bit of business during the tourist season. Daddies took their kiddies to the park for the rides and then found alternate entertainment for themselves. I knew this girl because I had treated her for gonorrhea on Friday.

"Hello, Annie," I said. "What can I do for you? Trouble with your medication?"

"Uh, no, it's okay," she said and looked at Paul, who looked at me and back to her. I was confused.

"Doctor Mullins, could I talk to you a minute, outside?" she asked and was on her way to the door.

Even more confused than before, I agreed and told Paul to make himself comfortable. By the time I closed the door, Annie had walked off the porch and was standing in the middle of the front walk.

"Okay, Annie, what's the trouble?"

"I'm so embarrassed. I didn't know you were his father."

I had assumed that the simultaneous arrival of Paul and Annie was coincidental. I was wrong. "What's going on?" I demanded.

"It's so embarrassing, and I wouldn't have done it if I knew it was you," she repeated.

"Come on, Annie. What are you talking about?"

"Well, you know how you told me not to work for three weeks?" She paused and when I nodded, she continued, "Well, that means that I'm the receptionist at the parlor, which is okay, but I'm not getting much money, you know."

I nodded again, and Annie searched for something imaginary in the pocket of her shorts. "Well, when this guy came in and asked if I wanted to make some money without, you know, screwing, I said sure. I didn't know he was your son. I didn't know you had a son."

"Paul came to see you? Does he know you?"

"Never saw him before. Anyway, he said he wanted to play a trick on his old man and wanted me to act like his wife. He said his old man hadn't seen him for a while, and he wanted to shock him. He wanted me to say I was part black, too."

"Oh," I asked stupidly, "are you?"

"Some, on my mother's side, but I'm mixed with just about everything. Look, like I said, I wouldn't have done it if I knew it was you. You're always nice to us girls when we have problems, and we all think that you're okay."

"Thanks," I said absently. "Why would Paul do that?"

Annie adjusted her halter. Her breast rose slightly, and I could see the nipple outlined beneath the fabric. Both her hair and eyes were black, and her limbs and midriff well tanned, and I didn't doubt that she had black ancestry. Her figure was voluptuous, but the plump of the stomach over her shorts suggested that figure could turn to fat. "I don't know, Doc. I guess you'll have to ask him."

"Yeah, I guess I'd better." I brought my attention back to Annie. "Thanks for telling me, and I'm sorry you got involved. Did he pay you?" My hand moved to my wallet.

"Keep it," she said. "I got some up front, and I'm not taking your money."

"Okay. You have a ride back?"

"Car's down the street. You're not upset with me are you, Doc?"

"Upset?" I asked vaguely. "No, I'm not upset with you. Just kind of confused is all."

"I know the feeling," Annie said. "Well, 'bye."

"'Bye," I said. "And keep taking those pills and let me check you before you go back to work."

She raised her hand in acknowledgment and blended into the dusk with her white shorts marking her progress to the car. I watched the shorts and wondered how in God's name I was going to handle this.

My first reaction was indignant anger, and I wanted to rant and rave at Paul. My second feeling was self pity, and I wanted to plead with Paul to respect the sacrifices I had made for him and for him to love me for those sacrifices. Thankfully, by the time I reached the door I had rejected both approaches and entered vowing to be as rational as possible.

Paul was having difficulty making himself comfortable. He had turned on the television, but wasn't watching it; he had been to the kitchen and left the light burning, and he changed his position on the sofa twice as I crossed to my chair. Annie was right; I hadn't seen him for a long time. His upper lip sported a small mustache, his hair was shorter and combed differently, and, to my consternation, he had a gold stud in his left ear.

"Annie had to go home early," I said.

Paul looked at the television. "Did she say anything?"

"Not much. She did mention that she was the new Mrs. Mullins, she was expecting to deliver twins in November, and that you and she rented a house on Oak Street. That's all."

Paul jerked his head from the television and rubbed his mustache. "She didn't say all that." He paused. "Did she?"

I swallowed the rest of my brandy. "No, but you need to be careful who you start telling tales to. Besides, Paul, as I have been reminded lately, this is a small town, and everyone pretty much knows about everyone else. Now, if you had brought one of your big city Minnesota whores, I might have been fooled."

Paul looked back to the television.

"Why'd you do all this, Paul?"

He shrugged. "I don't know. Just a prank."

"Bullshit. A prank is when you ring the doorbell and hide in the bushes, not pretend to be married to shock your old man, who, incidentally, isn't that damned old." My voice had risen.

Paul shifted his position on the couch again. "Mom said you were really pissed about the car. I thought maybe this would take your mind off it."

I laughed in spite of my anger. "You were right about that. I haven't thought about it once. You drive it here?"

"Yeah, it's out front."

I glanced at the window. "It's pretty dark now. I'll look at it in the morning."

"You're not pissed about it?"

"Paul, you're twenty-two years old. I guess if you want to buy a car, you can. I would have preferred that you used the money for college and that you talked to me about it first, but I guess it was your choice."

Paul looked pained. "Mom said I had to finish college. She told me to get the money from you."

"Paul, I simply don't have it. It's not a matter of my being angry with you. I just don't have any more money to give you."

"She's going to be mad."

"Won't be the first time," I muttered.

Paul shifted his position once more. "She said that you'd try to weasel out, that you had plenty of money."

"Well, she's wrong. I work for the county, and counties don't pay much. I couldn't afford the car you bought. By the way, why did you choose a BMW?" I asked, attempting to change the subject.

"I don't know, really. It just kind of happened. Mom and I were looking at cars one day, and we liked this one. A salesman offered us a discount, and I had deposited your check the day before. The next thing I knew, we were driving home. I asked Mom about college, but she said it would all work out."

"Whose name is the car in?" I asked, knowing the answer.

"Mom's. That way the insurance is cheaper."

"Did she sign the loan paper, too?" I knew the answer to that as well.

"She started to, but she had a couple of problems with her credit. If I signed them we could get a better interest rate."

Maria was good, I had to admit. She could and would manipulate anyone. Unlike Paul, I usually knew when it happened. I couldn't stop it, but at least I knew it. I felt sorry for Paul and was pissed at her.

"Staying a few days?" I asked, hoping for a more pleasant conversation.

Paul shrugged. "I guess I can."

"Good. Look, we can't settle anything tonight. I've got an early shift tomorrow, and I'm beat. Let's plan on dinner tomorrow."

Paul shrugged again. "I guess."

"I'll probably be gone before you get up, but I should be home by five. You can cruise around in your new car and impress the local girls." I was heading for my bedroom. "Use the extra room. There are some sheets in the dresser drawer, and I'll see you tomorrow for dinner. Oh, and Paul," I grinned at him, "try not to get married again tomorrow."

Paul looked up and grinned back. I felt a little better.

CHAPTER SIX

My shift began at six, and I left the house at five-thirty. Paul was still asleep, and I pulled the sheet over him. I smoothed it and realized that I was tucking in a grown man, and that I seldom had the chance to tuck in the boy. Life wasn't fair, I thought as I closed the bedroom door.

Paul's car was in front of the house, and in the pre-dawn light its chrome framed a shiny, dark body. I remembered that Maria had said that it was dark green. I peered through the tinted windows at the leather seats and a flashing alarm light. The trunk bore the number 740IL, which I knew was one of their best models and cost almost as much as two houses in Bishop. I shook my head and walked to my van. Maria didn't waste her skills on second-rate goods.

***

Within the first couple of hours on duty I treated the week-end disasters, which consisted of two ear infections, a nasty case of sunburn, and a sprained ankle. Without exception these maladies belonged to tourists, who were trying too hard to have fun. After the sprained ankle hobbled out, the ER was empty, and I called the University of Iowa and asked for the head of the anthropology department. After speaking to four secretaries and spending several minutes on hold, a Doctor Jacobs came on the line. I explained the situation and the necessity of a forensic anthropologist. Doctor Jacobs explained that he was a temporary faculty member teaching a summer class. He did, however, remember that one of his graduate professors did have forensic skills and occasionally assisted in the identity of skeletal remains. He promised to look up his name and number in the college directory when his class was over. As soon as I replaced the receiver, I became impatient for the call. If there was anything I hated more than being disturbed by calls, it was waiting for calls.

Knowing that Doctor Jacobs wouldn't phone for at least two or three hours, I phoned Bird. Mary wasn't at the switchboard, and the call was routed to Bird's house. His wife, Patty, informed me that he was asleep. Patty and Bird had been high school sweethearts and were married after graduation. The marriage was successful and both had established careers; Patty was the bookkeeper for most of the local businesses. Ten years ago they started a family, and they now had two daughters.

"I'm not waking him up, either," she said. "All he did yesterday was keep people out of that hotel and answer questions. Honestly, you'd think they could be satisfied with an official statement, but no, they all want more and exclusive interviews. I'm about to disconnect the phone." She paused to catch her breath. "How about you?" she asked. "They got to you, yet?"

"No, not yet."

"Huh," she grunted. "They will."

"Yeah, I know, but then I'm not as nice and friendly as Bird."

"You're right there. Bird has the patience of Job." She realized her mistake and apologized. "I don't mean that you're not nice, too, Bill."

"That's all right. I know I'm not. Tell Bird when he gets up that I got the pictures developed, the skeletons laid out for examination, and a line on a forensic anthropologist."

"I will," she said. "Is this guy going to give us some answers?"

"If anyone can, it would be him. Tell Bird I'll be at the hospital until about four if he wants me."

Doctor Jacobs proved himself a man of his word and called before noon with the name and number of a Doctor Owen Learner, who, according to Doctor Jacobs, could read bones like most people read the newspaper. The area code indicated that he lived in the central part of the state, and I placed a call. Doctor Learner answered by identifying himself in a soft voice, listened to my explanation without interruption, agreed that his services were needed, and excused himself while he checked his calendar. He returned to the phone and inquired if Wednesday would be satisfactory, since he had a dental appointment the next day. I assured him that was fine, and gave him both Bird's and my numbers and directions.

I decided that I liked Doctor Learner. No red tape, no unnecessary questions, and prompt service. I only hoped that he could answer the necessary questions.

Bird appeared in the ER near the end of my shift and sprawled on an examination table. "God, I'm beat," he announced.

"You look it. You in for treatment or passing time?"

"Hiding out, I guess. Patty said you called this morning. That news report yesterday really brought people out. Couple more television crews arrived. One's from Omaha. I forget where the other one's from. Bunch of newspaper reporters. I suspect they'll all be around until we tell them something definite. Speaking of which, how you coming along with answers?"

"I'm not, but I contacted an anthropologist. He'll be here Wednesday."

"Swell, that's sooner than I thought. The guy any good?"

"Supposed to be world class."

Bird grunted, "I hope so. Hope he works fast, too. I'm sick of giving the same answers to the same questions over and over."

"How's Ervin handling all this new competition?"

"That shithead. He's convinced that those skeletons were prisoners who were tortured in our jail and sealed to conceal the crimes of the previous administration."

I snickered, and Bird said, "Don't laugh. He's dead serious and will print it. At least he thinks it happened in the previous administration, not mine."

"Ervin's been sniffing printer's ink too long. Come on. I'll show you what I've done."

Bird pushed himself off the table and followed me to the morgue. He stopped at the door and looked at the room full of bones. "They are real. I thought more than once that I was dreaming it all."

"No such luck," I said.

"What happens now?" he asked.

"Nothing, until the anthropologist arrives."

"Anyone know they're here?"

"Not really. Nobody comes to the morgue much."

"What about the pictures? Patty said you developed them."

"Yeah, I've got them in my kit in the van. They're organized by the arrangement of the skeletons as we found them. The first two are on the right," I gestured. "The ones from the second room are on the left, and the third pair are down front. The fetus is on the autopsy table."

"Press bothered you yet?"

"Not yet. Saw a guy from WHO give me the eye, though."

"Yeah, well, just tell them we found six skeletons that were sealed up in the hotel. Don't mention the fetus. If they push you, refer them to me."

"Sure, Bird. You didn't say anything about the fetus?"

"No. I don't want this to get too sensational."

I nodded, although it seemed pretty sensational anyway. I looked at my watch. "Bird, I told Paul we'd go to dinner. I'm going to lock up unless you need something else."

"Nope. Have a good time and tell Paul hello. I'm going home to get an early dinner so I can spell Jim. See you."

"See you," I said, and closed the morgue, stuck a cigar in my mouth, and walked to the van, whose interior was unbearable. I let the air conditioner blow some of the hot air out the window. When the temperature became tolerable, I reached for the window crank, but instead had a microphone shoved in my face.

"Doctor Mullins, I'm Scott Christen, WHO TV News, and I have a few questions."

Scott Christen was the same young, blond reporter I'd seen at Emma's. Behind him was an equally young man with a video camera on his shoulder. It seemed to me that most of the world was young these days. I braced myself for the questions.

"First of all, are you the ME for Bishop?"

"That's right."

"And you agree to the interview?"

I nodded. I might as well get it over with.

Scott cued his cameraman and announced that he was conducting an exclusive interview with Bishop's medical examiner. Scott talked fast and faltered on a couple of words, which would probably prevent him from attaining an anchor position.

Scott fired the first question. "Can you describe what was found in the hotel, Doctor Mullins?"

He pushed the microphone too close to my face, and I backed away. Scott might not make it as a field reporter, either. "There were several skeletons found in sealed rooms."

"How many skeletons?"

"Six."

"Two per room?"

"That's right." I had revealed all the information that I was permitted to, and I hoped the interview was over.

Scott, however, was not finished. "What were the conditions of the bones?"

"Conditions?"

"Were they chewed or sharpened or anything like that?"

"No, nothing like that," I said.

"Were there sacrificial altars or devil worship signs in the hotel?"

"No."

"What about the cause of death? Were they tortured?"

"I'm not able to say."

"Why not?"

"Forensic anthropology is not my field. A specialist in that area will be examining the skeletons soon."

"Who is he? When will he examine them?"

Scott, I decided, might make it as an investigative reporter, and I knew I was being pumped for information. "I'm sorry, but Sheriff Starling will have to answer those questions." I turned away and put the van in gear.

Scott was tenacious. He followed the van as I backed out of the parking space and kept the microphone in my face. "Where are the skeletons now?"

"See Sheriff Starling," I said and drove towards the exit.

Scott started running. "Do you have pictures? Where are the pictures?"

I reached the street and accelerated away from Scott, who was directing his cameraman to film my retreating van. I had no idea how any of this would look on the news, but I was certain that Scott would show it in the worst possible context.

**

Bishop has one nice restaurant called Verne's, which is housed in a restored Victorian mansion amid oak trees on the edge of town. Two spinster sisters had once occupied the mansion, which had been built by their father in the lavish style of the robber barons of the nineteenth century. He had been a minor robber baron himself and controlled the railroad lines and freight in northwest Iowa. When the sisters died, their nephew acquired it, and began to restore it. The restaurant was added to defray the cost of the restoration. Verne's became known for quality food and service, and was patronized by citizens of four counties.

Paul guided the BMW up the drive and glanced around. "This is pretty nice," he said. "Better than I expected."

"Has a great view from the top. Since it's a week day, we

should be able to get a window seat. Place is usually packed on the weekends. Let's use the valet parking and impress the attendants with your car."

The attendant whisked the BMW off with no more appreciation than if it had been a pickup truck. Paul and I crossed the massive porch to the entrance. The porch had tables for cocktails, but with the temperature in the nineties, people were taking advantage of the air conditioning. I opened the door for Paul.

"Do you come here a lot?" he asked.

"Hell, this is my second time. I know where the men's room is and everything."

Paul grinned. Twice in two days.

The hostess showed us to a window seat, presented us with menus and made suggestions. Verne's is known for its prime rib, which Paul ordered, but since I digest beef somewhat inefficiently, I opted for the grilled halibut. While we waited we admired the view which overlooked a valley of patchworked corn and bean fields.

"See that area over there beyond that big clump of trees?" I pointed.

"Yeah."

"Your great-grandfather homesteaded that land about eighty, ninety years ago. I remember visiting him before he died. I was just a little kid then."

"I think I saw his picture today. The one on the book shelf in the living room?"

"Yeah, that's right. The one next to it is my parents, your grandparents. My mother died when I was in high school, my father a few years ago."

"My grandfather didn't farm?"

I realized that Paul knew almost nothing about my family. "No, he hated farming and sold the land as soon as your great-grandfather died. Your granddad was a mechanic. A good one, too. I used to help him in the summers when I was in high school. Learned a lot."

"You can fix cars?" Paul asked.

"Well, not these new ones where everything is electronic and computerized, but I can handle most stuff on a plain old motor. I'll show you my Mercury when we get home. Rebuilt it myself."

"Where's the lake? I've been hearing about that and some skeletons all day long."

"It's on the north side of town," I turned to point and was blinded by a bright light. "What the hell?"

"Doctor Mullins? Scott Christen. We didn't get to finish our interview, and I have some more questions."

I blinked several times until I could see Scott's blond hair. "You damn near blinded me."

"Sorry. Now, where are the skeletons, and when will the pictures be made public?"

"Oh for chrissake, I'm having dinner," I protested.

"About the skeletons and the pictures, Doctor?"

"See Sheriff Starling and get the hell out of here."

"Doctor Mullins, is it true you left California because of incompetence?"

I snapped my head to face him and locked in on his blue eyes. "No, it's not true, but since you went to so much trouble to find out about me, you probably found out what I've done to reporters, and every word of that is true." I edged forward on my chair, and Scott stepped back. Fortunately, he stepped back into the arms of two waiters, who ushered him and his cameraman outside.

The hostess offered apologies, the waiter brought our orders, and we settled into dinner. Halfway through his prime rib Paul asked, "You didn't leave because of incompetence, did you?"

"Hell, no. I left because I was burnt out. Wanted a slower pace. I was damned good at what I did."

"What exactly did you do?"

"Same thing that I do now. I'm an emergency room doctor, and I handle whatever problems arrive at the hospital's doors. In Los Angeles that usually included shootings, stabbings, overdoses, accidents, things like that. I was good at it. You get shot, stabbed, or thrown through a windshield, and I'm your man. You get cancer, liver disease, or something like that and you want somebody else."

"Do I have to have any of those?" Paul grinned. *Three times in two days.*

Chapter Seven

Tuesday set a high temperature record and the humidity pressed the heat down like a wet blanket. Air conditioners started humming and spewing puddles of water beneath them in the early morning. Locals stayed within the confines of those air conditioners whenever possible and limited their activities to mopping sweat and sipping lemonade. A few tourists stubbornly refused to sacrifice golf and water skiing to the weather. I treated three cases of heat exhaustion before noon.

Bird arrived after lunch, helped himself to a cold pack from the refrigerator, and sprawled on an examination table.

"Hotter than the hubs of hell out there," he said.

"Yup."

"You see the news this morning?"

"No, I don't watch television much."

Bird snorted under the cold pack. "Well, you missed your screen debut. Dandy scene of you threatening a defenseless reporter."

"What?"

"Oh, yeah," he continued, "whole town's abuzz. Emma's

bragging that you buy your sandwiches from her. Boys at the Golden Eagle are calling you Rambo. The mayor, however, has a little different perspective."

"Oh, shit," I said.

"Oh, shit is right. You and I are having a meeting with him as soon as your shift ends. I'll pick you up." Bird sat up and removed the cold pack. "You just can't stay out of trouble, can you?"

"Damn, Bird, I didn't do anything. That punk reporter was bugging me during dinner. I told him to get lost. Couple of waiters tossed him out. Not me."

"Not the way it looks on tape. Looks like you deserve the name Rambo."

"Hell, I never even touched the guy. I just told him to get lost."

"Hey, I believe you, but then I know you. Since you're kind of an enigma around town, people are going to believe what they see. I dealt with Scott Christen a couple years back; he went to the Ervin Johnston school of journalism. He wants the sensational headlines and will play fast and loose with the facts to get them. You gave him one last night: 'Medical Examiner Assaults Reporter.'"

"I don't know how in the hell this kind of stuff happens to me. I mind my business, do my job, and the next thing I know some little shit has got my face all over television."

"Yeah," said Bird, "newspapers, too, probably. But hey, most people think you did the right thing. I personally think you should have shoved the camera up his ass. But like I said, the mayor has a different perspective." Bird wiped the cold pack around his neck. "Well, better get back into that oven and see how Jim's getting along. Only thing good about this heat is that it's keeping people away from the hotel."

"Hey, Bird, Scott had a lot of questions about where the skeletons are and the pictures we took. How'd he know we took pictures or even moved them, for that matter? You say something to him?"

"Hell, no. As for moving them, he probably guessed. Maybe he guessed about the pictures, too. It would be a usual procedure. Maybe Jim said something, but I doubt it. He was pretty interested, you say?"

"Yeah, persistent is the word. I figure he wants to be the first to broadcast the pictures."

"No doubt. That would be Scott's style. Where are the pictures now?"

"In my kit in the van."

"Better let me put them in the safe in my office just to be sure."

By the time Bird and I walked to my van the collar of my shirt was wet, and I could feel the heat of the asphalt through the soles of my shoes. The inside of the van was intolerable, and I snatched the bundle of pictures from the kit and handed them to Bird. He was striding to his patrol car when a thought hit me.

"Should we check them first?" I asked.

Bird stopped and wiped a trickle of sweat from his cheek. "Might just be a good idea."

We retreated to the ER and air conditioning. Bird started thumbing through the pictures.

"Don't mix them up," I said. "They're all in order for Doctor Learner."

"Who?"

"The forensic anthropologist who's arriving tomorrow."

"Oh, yeah. Well, how can we tell if they're all here?"

"Count, I guess. I used three rolls of film with thirty-six exposures each so that's a hundred and eight, but there were ten exposures left on the last roll. That's ninety-eight. I made two set of prints, so there should be a hundred and ninety-six pictures and ninety-eight negatives."

"Okay," said Bird, "let's count."

We counted three times to the correct number of pictures, but to only ninety-seven negatives.

Bird tapped his fingers on the table. "No mistake about it: one negative's gone. You keep the van locked?"

"Yeah, all the time. Kit, too."

"Looks like our buddy Scott has some skills we didn't know about."

"Think it was him?" I asked.

"Seems like a good suspect right now. Trouble is proving it."

"Fingerprints?"

"I'll dust, but I'll bet he wore gloves."

I watched Bird dust and lift fingerprints off the van's doors and the kit. "I'll check, but they're probably yours, mine, and Jim's." He ran his handkerchief around his face and neck. "Blast furnace in there."

I sat on the edge of the side step and wondered how one little shit could make my life so miserable. First, he accosted me, then made out that I had attacked him, and now evidence entrusted to me was missing. I anticipated an uncomfortable meeting with the mayor. I was reaching over the seat for a cigar from the glove compartment when I saw it. At the base of the seat directly behind my kit the sunlight illuminated a blond hair as it does when it hits the silver strands of a spider's web.

"Bird," I said, and extracted the hair with tweezers and put it in an evidence bag. "We may not need fingerprints."

Bird squinted into the bag. "It's a hair. So what?"

"A hair can tell about anything you want to know about a person, including his DNA, and what he ingests. Each person's hair is unique, and will match to that person as accurately as fingerprints."

"Damn, all right. How'd you know that?"

"I've been to the big city, my man," I said, which was basically true. Several times I had taken samples from under the nails of beating and rape victims for detectives. I hadn't used that procedure in Bishop since there had been no such victims in recent memory.

"How long would it take to identify that as Scott's hair?" Bird asked.

"I'm not sure exactly," I said.

"What do you mean?"

"Well, I know it can be done, but I didn't say I knew how to do it. We could send it to the FBI crime lab in Des Moines, but we'd need another hair for comparison—"

"Aw, shit," Bird flapped his arms. "That takes time. I want to get him before we see the mayor." He glanced at his watch. "But that's not likely. We're due there in ten minutes. Lock up and I'll drive you."

***

The mayor was a member of a founding family that was now one of the richest, with several thousand acres of farm land distributed among its members. They also had investments in meat packing, cement and gravel, implement manufacturing, and lately, genetic engineering. The Ellerbrock family was more diversified than most countries. His individual wealth had allowed Michael Ellerbrock to serve as mayor for almost twenty years without drawing a salary, which was one of his campaign slogans, "The Best for Free."

Although the mayor worked for free, he did so in opulent surroundings. His private office was at least three times the size of my living room, paneled in cherrywood, and adorned with original watercolors. His desk matched the paneling and was large enough to park a car on. The rest of the room was furnished with a leather couch and wing-back chairs. It reminded me more of an elegant hotel lobby than an office.

Mayor Ellerbrock was as large as his office with wisps of white hair that mingled with the wisps of smoke from his ever-present pipe. At Christmas he played a believable Santa Claus for the elementary school children.

The aroma of pipe tobacco announced his arrival at his office where Bird and I were engulfed in wing-back chairs. Following him were Scott Christen and his cameraman. I groaned inwardly, and heard Bird mutter "shit" under his breath. The mayor sat behind his desk and worked his girth beneath the top. Scott and the cameraman settled on the couch; the latter fiddled with his camera. I groaned again; more film for tonight's newscast.

"Sheriff, Doctor," the mayor nodded, paused to relight his pipe, and focused his heavy-lidded eyes on me. "Mr. Christen and his associate have leveled some serious charges against you, Doctor, and frankly, having seen the video tape of the incident, I must say that I am appalled by your conduct. Your behavior did not represent your position as a professional county employee."

I've never liked the mayor much; he's too long-winded. I wasn't directly responsible to him anyway, since I worked for the county. I figured he'd recommend that the county board reprimand me. It wouldn't be my first.

Mayor Ellerbrock gestured with his pipe to Scott. "Mr. Christen is well within his rights to press charges against you for assault and bodily harm. He has graciously offered to accept your apology instead."

I understood the reason for the camera, now. My apology was going to be broadcast to all WHO and affiliate viewers. A letter of reprimand I could stand, but I wasn't about to humble myself in front of this punk while half the midwest watched.

"Mr. Ellerbrock, at no time have I threatened or touched Mr. Christen or his faithful companion. I'm sure you're aware that video tapes can be creatively edited, and my behavior can be verified by Verne's staff. Also, Mr. Ellerbrock, it is my duty to report to you that some evidence, specifically a film negative relating to the skeletons found in the hotel, has been stolen. I believe that Mr. Christen appropriated that evidence and that he plans to broadcast that evidence on tonight's news show and scoop the other networks. He'll probably claim it came from a source close to the investigation."

I was sweating in the cool air. I saw Bird squeezing the bridge of his nose with his thumb and forefinger, but I had gone too far to stop.

The mayor waved at some smoke. "Outrageous."

"Hey, man, I never appropriated nothing," said Scott and sniffed his nose.

I disliked people without manners. "It may be outrageous, Mr. Ellerbrock," I said, looking squarely at him, "but the sheriff and I found evidence that put Mr. Christen at the scene of the crime."

"Hah," snorted Scott. "Like what did you find? My fingerprints?" He snickered and sniffed.

I knew I was right about him taking the negative, and

Bird was right about him wearing gloves. Scott was talking faster and tripping over more words than usual. I knew I was right about something else.

I turned and locked onto Scott's blue eyes. He blinked and I pressed. "Mr. Christen, do you know why criminals wear nylon stockings over their heads?"

Scott looked confused. "Sure, so nobody recognizes them."

"Absolutely correct. You were probably a joy to your parents." I couldn't resist the sarcasm. "But not entirely correct. They also do it to keep from leaving strands of hair at inopportune places. You forgot to do that, and you left this hair in my van." I produced the evidence bag from my pocket and shoved it in his face.

Scott drew back perceptively, then recovered. "You can't prove that's my hair."

I smiled. "Right again, Scott my boy. I'll bet you did real well in school. But all we need to do is compare it to a sample from your head to let the truth be known." I extended my arm towards him. He shifted away and bumped into his cameraman.

I dropped my hand. "But the best part, Scott, is still to come, and you may want Cecil B. DeMille there to line up his camera."

The cameraman raised his view finder to his eye; Scott pushed the camera down. At least, I thought, he's taking me seriously.

"You see, Scott, hair can tell lots of stuff about a person. What he eats, vitamins he takes, medications. All that leaves a residue in hair. You might be interested to know that this hair here—" I waved it in his face again, "this hair is just full of cocaine, which, of course, means that its owner has a healthy habit and probably has some on his person right now."

Bird took his cue and stood up. The mayor made harumphing sounds. Scott's eyes were on the floor, and his cameraman moved to the opposite side of the couch, and spoke his only words, "Told you, big shot."

"Scott," I said. "Let's save us all from embarrassment. Why don't you get your editor on the phone and tell him to kill that story you got with the negative and anything connected with it. I also want any tapes, pictures, or recordings that you have of me. I think you could get everything in Sheriff Starling's possession in a couple of hours. After that, I think you ought to get your shit-eatin' face out of the county."

I sat in the chair and gripped the arms so my hands wouldn't shake. Scott called his editor and whimpered to him awhile; Bird took the phone to convey the seriousness of the matter, and escorted Scott and his companion to his office. He gave me a quick thumbs up as he left the room.

The mayor relit his pipe and waved at the smoke. "I apparently owe you an apology."

"Yes," I said, "and I accept it."

The mayor nodded; the matter was resolved to his satisfaction. "That was quite a performance. Can hair really tell that much about a person?"

"Oh, yeah. Pretty much whatever is in you comes out in your hair."

The mayor puffed. "Would smoke be in my hair?"

"The nicotine and tars would be," I answered. "So would the caffeine from your coffee."

"I'll be damned. Did you find anything else in Mr. Christen's hair?"

I shifted in the chair. "Actually, I don't have the equipment for those types of tests. I would have to send it to a crime lab."

"But you had the hair—" He stopped and pulled the pipe from his mouth. "Do you mean to tell me that this whole thing was a bluff? You had no evidence at all?"

"Well, I did have the hair. I guess the rest was pretty much a bluff."

The mayor chuckled, then laughed. I could hear his belly hitting the top desk drawer. The laugh turned into a wheezing cough, and he slapped himself a few times in the chest. "You should have seen his face," he rasped, forgetting that I had been there. "He looked like he pissed his pants at the prom. Bill, there's more to you than meets the eye. You don't say much, but when you do, look out."

Not knowing what to say, I mumbled "Thanks" and made excuses to leave. The mayor, still chuckling and wheezing, nodded and waved me to the door. I heard, "Pissed his pants at the prom," followed by a paroxysm of coughing as I closed the door.

CHAPTER EIGHT

Paul was sprawled across the couch wearing only his underwear. He looked up from the television and announced that I needed air conditioning.

"I agree, but it does get cooler on the porch after the sun sets. I sit out there quite a bit. What'd you do today?"

"Not much. Drove around some because the car has air conditioning. Went by that old hotel. What's the deal on that? I've heard all kinds of stuff."

I explained to Paul about the skeletons and the sealed rooms.

"Jeez, that's weird," he said. "Were they sealed up a long time?"

"My guess is yes. Once the anthropologist examines the bones we should know how long they were in there."

"Any idea who they were and who sealed them up?"

"Nope to both. May not ever know. I think Bird wants to believe that Nate Griswold was behind it, but that's just because it would be convenient. Nate used to own the hotel, and he's dead, so there wouldn't be anything like a jury trial. I don't think he had anything to do with it, though. He was old when he bought the place, and his health wasn't too good, either. Besides, I knew Nate a little. He used to hang around my dad's garage once in a while. He seemed more interested in gin rummy and telling stories than in killing people. But you never can tell. What do you want for dinner?"

"Something cool," Paul said.

Besides Verne's, Bishop boasted four other eateries, including the drug store that offered microwaved hot dogs, fish sticks, and macaroni and cheese. The Dairy Queen served hamburgers and fries along with its ice milk creations. The Uptown Cafe, so named because it was across the street from the court house, was operated by its original owner, whose dimmed eyes were oblivious to the grime and who believed that everything should be fried in lard. Emma's Deli offered only sandwiches and potato salad, but the portions were generous, it was clean, and most important today, air conditioned.

After our dinner at Emma's, Paul and I treated ourselves to ice cream cones at the Dairy Queen and later sat on my front porch watching the dusk turn the sky steel blue and fill in the shadows.

"See," I said, "it does get cooler out here when the sun goes down." I was on my second glass of brandy and at that moment felt at ease with the world.

"I don't know if cool is the word," said Paul, "but it is tolerable." He rubbed his mustache. "Mom called today," he announced.

"Oh, what did she want?" I asked. My pleasant mood began to evaporate.

"Well, mostly she wanted to know what I had worked out with the money and when I was coming home."

"Uh-huh. What did you tell her?"

"I said that you and I hadn't talked about it much yet. She told me to get it settled fast and get the car back."

I detected a little annoyance in Paul's voice, and I decided to probe. "Did you and your mother work out an agreement about the use of the car?"

"Not really," he said. "She just said she might want to use it sometimes."

"Sometimes" to Maria meant whenever she wanted it. I probed a little more. "Think she'll be using it quite a bit?"

"Yeah," Paul said quietly. "I'm not stupid, and I know this isn't the greatest deal for me, but Mom kind of swept me along."

"Don't feel bad. I've been there. Let me ask you another question: you still want to live with your mother, or would you be happier on your own?"

"I think I'd like to try it on my own."

"I think you're right. Anyone your age would have a hard time living at home. I know I wouldn't have been able to do it."

"Mom's all right and everything, but ..."

"But you want to live your own life," I finished.

"Right. But how's that going to happen? I'm not done with school, and I can't pay for the car and support myself at the same time."

"Well," I said, "I've been giving that some thought. I got an acquaintance that runs a car auction in Sioux City. I talked to him, and he thinks he could get a pretty good price for the BMW. You'd probably lose most of that down payment, but you wouldn't have payments to contend with. And you kind of know you've got to sell it, don't you?"

I saw Paul nod in the shadows. "But I do need a car," he said.

"Thought about that, too. I got another acquaintance in Des Moines that runs a salvage yard. Sometimes he gets some pretty good cars, maybe because somebody's great aunt died and nobody wanted to mess with her old car. Anyway, he has a couple of those, a Chevy Nova and a Comet that he'd sell for three hundred dollars. Now, you'd have to put on new brakes, hoses, a seal or two, but they both run. You could probably put together a solid car for under a thousand. Not a pretty car, but one suitable for transportation."

I looked at Paul to see if he was showing any distaste to the idea of giving up the best and accepting the passable. His face was impassive.

"That's all well and good," he said, "but how would that get me out on my own?"

"Thought about that, too, and all I can do is make a suggestion. Without that car payment you could afford to support yourself and maybe save a little money. I thought you could get a job for a semester or so and save some money to go back to college. By that time I ought to have gotten some money together again, and I can help you out." I made a push. "You might find a job around here. Those resorts by the lake hire all through the summer. The elevator usually needs extra help during harvests, and there's an implement repair place on the highway. Rent's pretty cheap in town." I made another push. "Or you could stay here until you find something."

Paul grinned, "I was hoping you'd come up with something. Now, are you going to tell Mom?"

"Yeah," I said quickly before I had time to think about it. "But you have to back me up. If she senses any weakness in your resolve, it's all over."

Paul nodded. "Dad, I really don't know how to change brakes or hoses or whatever."

I liked the "Dad." I smiled. "It's time you learned, son. It's time you learned."

Paul asked me to get him up when I left for the ER in the morning in order to get an early start in applying for jobs. I went to bed amazed that Paul had made the decisions that I had not really hoped for in my wildest dreams. I had not expected him to give up the BMW without a fight, and I certainly didn't think he'd want to live in Bishop with me. Yet he seemed genuinely pleased with that very prospect. Twenty years after my divorce, my son was going to live with me. I knew that at his age Paul wouldn't stand for much fathering, but the idea that we would be together and he might seek my advice made me feel less alone when I turned out my light and settled into the darkness.

Chapter Nine

Doctor Owen Learner arrived at the ER at eleven o'clock, accompanied by Bird and Mayor Ellerbrock. He looked like his voice: soft and unoffending. He had a slight build, which, despite the heat, was covered with a starched white shirt, red tie, and black suit with a vest. His Phi Beta Kappa key hung from a gold chain that stretched from a buttonhole to his pocket. He wore rimless glasses held together with strips of gold, and what hair he had left was cut to the skin. His mouth flinched upward in what I took to be a smile, and he shook my hand with tapered fingers that flattened at the end. He had a surprisingly strong grip and an odd tic: at frequent intervals his left arm flinched and banged its elbow against his ribs.

The mayor was harumphing his throat clear to say something unnecessary, and Doctor Learner anticipated him. "Would it be possible, Doctor Mullins, to view the skeletons?"

"Absolutely, Doctor," I said, pleased to avoid the mayor's banalities. "Just follow me."

"Christ Almighty," was the mayor's only comment when I opened the door to the morgue. Fortunately, as far as I was concerned, his first encounter with the skeletons had rendered him almost speechless.

Doctor Learner was likewise quiet, but busy. I saw his eyes darting behind his lenses as he appraised the situation. "Small room," he said. "Not much room to work."

"You have the entire pathology lab available to you," I explained.

Learner nodded, and his arm twitched a couple of times. "Mayor Ellerbrock, I believe that I have approximately two day's work here and a third day to prepare my report. I have discussed my daily fee with you. Also, I cannot perform all the tests here, but I am able to use the lab at the university. They will exact a payment from you." His arm twitched and he fingered his Phi Beta Kappa key. "If that is satisfactory, I can begin immediately."

"Yes, by all means," said the mayor. "Bill," I was on a first name basis after yesterday afternoon, "would you assist Doctor Learner? And Bird, I could use a ride back to my office." Mayor Ellerbrock propelled his bulk across the lab at a rate that surpassed Bird's stride.

"Well, Doctor, how can I assist you?" I asked. "Need equipment?"

"I brought my own. Perhaps you could help me transport it from my car?"

Doctor Learner's equipment consisted of a medical bag that he carried and an expandable file that he entrusted to me. He asked me questions about the skeletons and the hotel. I answered and explained my arrangement of the skeletons, the order of the pictures, and the bags of fibers and the bullet. He complimented me on my thoroughness, hung his jacket on the back of a chair, and opened his bag. I sensed that he had entered his comfortable world of bones, and I returned to the ER.

By the end of my shift, I was more than a little curious, and I detoured through the morgue. Doctor Learner had wheeled two of the skeletons, the two from the first room, into the lab and was peering at the skull of one through a magnifying glass. He glanced at me, and I caught a distorted image of his cheek and eye through the glass.

"Doctor," he said, both as a greeting and an address. His arm twitched. "Could you assist me a moment?"

"Sure, I guess. But I'm not very familiar with this field."

His mouth flinched into his smile. "Nothing complicated. I need you to hold the tape while I measure some bones."

"I can manage that," I said, and moved closer to the table.

Learner had returned his attention to the skull. "Fine. Would you retrieve the tape from my bag, please? I'll be finished here momentarily."

We measured the femurs, tibias, and fibulas of both skeletons, and he recorded the results and referred to some charts in his expandable file. He recorded some more numbers and said, "Thank you, young man. You were most helpful."

I liked being called "young man," but not being left in the dark. "Uh, Doctor, could you tell me what we just did?"

He looked at me as if I had asked in which direction the sun rose. He flinched a smile and said, "Of course. The leg bones, especially the femur," he patted the one closest to him, "gives the best indication of the person's height. Based on those measurements I would say that the female here," he pointed to the skeleton on the second table, "was quite short, no more than five feet. The male," he pointed to the first table, "was about five-eight."

I was intrigued. "How did you determine the sex?"

"Primarily by the pelvic bone," he said, and picked up the

one belonging to the female. "The opening is larger in females, for birthing purposes, obviously. Also, the sciatic notches," he turned the pelvis to afford a rear view, "are just a bit wider in females. The acetabulum, however," he turned the pelvis again to reveal the hip socket, "is a bit smaller." He put the pelvis down and reached for the skull, which he balanced on the palm of his hand, and directed my attention to its forehead. "The brow ridges on females are smaller than on males, as are the mastoid processes." He indicated the bone behind the ear. "You can compare these to the other skull if you want."

I did, and could clearly see the differences. "What else do you know?"

Learner sensed my interest and picked up the female's pelvis. "This lady bore at least one child. See that grove in the sulcus? That results from childbirth. I can't say when she gave birth or anything about the child, but she definitely had one."

He replaced the pelvis and picked up the left radius. I noticed that his tic had all but disappeared and behind his lenses, his eyes showed a glimmer of excitement. "See that ossification? This lady had a nasty broken arm when she was young. It didn't heal straight, either. You can see the misaligned bone. Also, notice the tiny cracks on the surface of the bone. They confirm your suspicion that the skeletons were imprisoned in the hotel for years. These cracks are caused by the bones freezing and thawing, and they are on every bone here."

"Why are the bones so dark?" I asked.

He frowned. "I'm not sure. Actually, most bones are dark, although these seem a bit darker than most. We tend to think of skeletons as being white, like the Halloween caricature. I suppose this is from the fact that most skeletons are found outside and the sun has bleached their bones. Bones that are exhumed are quite a different color. These were found in sealed rooms?"

"Yes."

"How sealed were they? I mean were the doors locked? Were there windows?"

"They were sealed well enough to hide the existence of the rooms themselves."

Learner frowned again. "No cracks or crevices to allow access to insects or small animals?"

"I don't think so."

"Well, their decomposition may have been much slower than usual. After death a body goes through several different changes, each of which can be used to suggest time of death." He paused, banged his elbow a couple of times, and decided he had an interested audience. "The first stage is lividity, where the blood pools to the lowest spot on the body, which causes purple discoloration. This starts within several minutes after death and becomes fixed with the discoloration set in about six hours. Rigor mortis begins about four hours after death and lasts for something over a day. By the end of a day the body has taken on a greenish color and a rotten smell is evident. In about three days gas from bacteria forms blisters on the body and the skin bursts. This process continues for several weeks, exposing the muscle tissues, and finally, the bones."

Doctor Learner banged his elbow and continued. "This process is influenced by two things: temperature and insects. The house fly, blow fly, bottle fly, green fly, or whatever you want to call it, is immediately attracted by death. An open wound attracts it faster. Within ten minutes a few flies can lay thousands of eggs in a body. In about twelve hours these eggs hatch as maggots and begin to feed on tissue. Beetles arrive two or three days later to feed on the loosened skin. They are followed by regiments of other insects, some of which feed on the body, some on the other insects. If the bodies of these skeletons were protected from all this, their decomposition would have been slower."

I nodded, feeling a little repulsed. "What about temperature?"

"Warm temperature speeds the process, and cold temperatures slow it, by several weeks in both cases. But I think we must consider that temperatures in Iowa as more than just warm and cold. In winter the bodies would have been frozen, which would have halted any decomposition. On a hot summer's day I suspect that the temperature in an un-vented, stagnant room could rise past a hundred and twenty degrees, which would have greatly accelerated the process."

I considered for a few moments. "So if the bodies were sealed in, say, late summer or fall, they would have been frozen, thawed, cooked, frozen, then cooked again?"

"Basically, that's how I see it, although it sounds unsavory. I think that those temperature extremes stained the bones and probably left that residue on the sheets."

"Good Christ," I mumbled.

Doctor Learner cleared his throat, and his elbow hit his ribs. "I was in the process of determining age. Would you like to assist?" he asked, and returned the conversation to a more comfortable level.

"How do you do that?"

He reached for a skull. "A combination of factors determine age. One is the thickness of the cranium. It is noticeably thinner in people of advanced age. This lady," he stroked the skull's forehead, "was not of advanced age. The degree of closure of the epiphyses between the cranial bones, and the teeth that show the eruption of all molars including wisdom teeth, would place her age roughly between twenty and fifty. These pits in the cranial bones suggest that she was well past twenty, and finally," he exchanged the skull for the pelvis and pointed to the pubic symphysis, "this little bone metamorphoses according to age. Judging from its condition, I would say this lady was in her mid-thirties when she died."

"This is amazing. I had no idea bones were so revealing."

Learner flinched a smile. "Only a few odd characters like myself are even interested. I'm afraid I talked through the dinner hour, and I must be keeping you from your family."

"No, I live—" I was about to say "alone" when my new parenting instincts stopped me. "My son is visiting me for a while. I guess I should see how he's doing."

"How old is your son?"

I didn't think Learner knew any personal questions. "Oh, he's twenty-two and can certainly take care of himself. It's just that he applied for some jobs today, and I wanted to see how he did."

"You are divorced?"

"Yeah, for years. Paul, my son, and I are kind of getting reacquainted. Listen, if you're done for the day, I'll wheel those two back into the morgue. We've had a little trouble with some overzealous reporters."

"Thank you. Will I be able to use the lab tomorrow?"

"Oh, sure. It doesn't get used much. Unless somebody dies suspiciously or there's an outbreak of food poisoning or cholera, it'll be empty. Besides, I'm the one who takes care of that stuff." I paused. "Uh, Doctor, if I'm not busy in the ER tomorrow, would you mind if I helped you again? I really find this fascinating."

"Of course. But may I ask what you do that gives you free time?"

"I work in the emergency room. It's usually routine stuff and pretty light. I'm the medical examiner, too, but that's pretty routine, too."

"I see."

"I worked the ERs in Los Angeles county hospitals for ten years," I said defensively. "That wasn't routine."

"I'm sure it wasn't." Doctor Learner had returned his equipment to his bag and had donned his jacket. "I wonder if you could recommend a restaurant?"

"We don't have too many choices, Doctor." I was certain that he would not appreciate the lard-infused fare of the Uptown Cafe. "The county paying your expenses?"

"Yes."

"Go to Verne's. You'll see a sign for it on Main Street."

"Thank you."

I was pushing the second table into the morgue, when I heard Doctor Learner call from across the room. I looked up.

"A young man needs a challenge," he said and stepped out the door.

I locked the morgue, feeling that my bones had just been read.

CHAPTER TEN

Paul was sprawled on the couch reading a bartender's guide.

"Taking up drinking?" I asked.

"No, but I did get a job. Two, in fact."

"Yeah? Great. Doing what?"

Paul sat up and rubbed his mustache. "I'm the new house-man for the Inn at the Pines Lodge. Got hired the second place I went."

"Swell. What's a houseman?"

His shoulders sagged a bit. "A janitor. The maids clean the rooms, and I clean everything else. Pays minimum, but it's a start."

"Sure it is. I was a houseman more than once myself, but I didn't get the fancy title." I was proud of Paul. He was willing to work at a job that many people would consider beneath them. "What's with the bartender's guide?"

"That's my second job. Mr. Jason, he's the manager, saw I was over twenty-one and asked if I could mix drinks. I can, a few anyway. He said that when they have conventions and catered dinners for clubs and businesses, they set up a host bar. The regular bartender can't take care of both, so Mr. Jason thought I could give it a try. He said the tips are pretty good, and there's a dinner scheduled for Friday for some club. I thought I better brush up a little."

"Sounds good. You had better luck than I expected. Must be good." I gave him a shot in the arm. He grinned. "You eat dinner?" I asked.

"Yeah, I ate at the lodge since I was there."

"I haven't. Guess I'll make some soup or something. I was helping with the skeletons this afternoon. I learned a lot. Amazing stuff."

"Yeah? Like what?" Paul asked. He had followed me to the kitchen where I was rummaging in the cabinets for something edible.

"Like how to tell a person's age and sex from his or her bones. Learned how to determine height by the leg bones. This guy, Doctor Learner, can read bones like you're reading that book. When he's done we should know quite a bit about those skeletons." I dumped some soup in a pan and hunted for crackers. "Except I don't figure that anyone can tell us why they were in that hotel, or what their names were." I added crackers to my soup and eased the bowl to my recliner. "You work tomorrow?"

"Yeah, early. I get weekends off unless I tend bar."

"Hey, good," I said with my mouth full of noodles. "Maybe we can get to Des Moines for your car. I'll see if I can get Johnny at the garage to rent me his flatbed hauler." I spooned soup into my mouth. "How do you want to handle this with your mother?"

Paul shrugged. "I don't know. Any suggestions?"

"A telegram," I said and wiped my chin with my finger and sighed. "I guess there's no point in procrastinating. We can call her when I finish eating." I looked Paul in the eye. "That is, if you're still going to back me up."

Paul nodded. "I will, Dad."

I dumped my bowl in the sink, poured half a glass of brandy, and dialed Maria's number. She answered in her cheerful, almost melodious tone, which became brittle when she determined who it was. I explained Paul's decision and my arrangements and requested the paperwork for the BMW. Maria responded with derisive remarks about my parenting abilities, manhood, and employment. I endured the tirade, and supported by the presence of my son, refused to back down. Maria demanded to speak to Paul, and I'm sure he was subjected to a similar display. I used my respite to sip brandy and gather strength for my next onslaught like a fighter revitalizes himself for the next round.

My next round never came. After ten minutes of interrupted explanations, Paul raised his voice and said, "Look, Mom, be honest. You want the car so you can impress younger guys. That's why you talked me into buying it. It wasn't for me at all." This was followed by many seconds of silence, and I assumed Maria was crying and lamenting her life's sacrifices. Paul talked quietly for a couple of minutes and said, "Yes, Mom, I think it's best. Of course I'll visit you, and of course I love you." He hung up and grinned at me.

"Boy," I said, "you play some hardball. I'd hate to have you mad at me."

"Well, it worked. Besides, it's true. I just liked the car so much that I tried to believe it really was for me."

I rolled my cigar to the other side of my mouth. "You mean your mother does date young guys?"

Paul sank onto the couch. "Yeah. Ever since her last divorce it's been a thing with her. She sometimes introduces me as her younger brother so her dates won't know how old she is."

"Jesus Christ," I said and touched my graying hair. "I guess I couldn't get away with that. Not that I especially want to date young girls."

"You don't look that old, Dad," he said. "And what's wrong with young girls? I date them."

"Yeah, *you're* young. Besides, they always want to talk to you."

"Don't older women want that, too?"

"Well, yeah. That's a problem with them, too."

Paul rolled his eyes. "You need to get out more, Dad."

"I suppose. Been busy, though."

"Yeah, right. Want me to fix you up?" His dark eyes danced in the light from the table lamp.

"Isn't that a switch," I said. "And just when did you become a mother? Be sure to tell any prospects that I'm a doctor. I'll be beating them off with a stick."

***

I opened the door to the morgue before I reported to the ER. Owen Learner was facing me when I turned around. I jumped back and bumped the wall.

"Jesus, you scared the shit out of me. I didn't think anybody was around this early."

Learner twitched his arm. "I'm sorry I startled you. I wanted to get in a full day of work." He was dressed identically to yesterday, except that today's tie was a deeper shade of red.

The dawn was sending its first light through the windows of the lab. "Yeah, well, you'll get that," I said. "You had breakfast?"

"The motel offered a continental breakfast."

"If you want some real food the cafeteria is your best bet. Just don't get the oatmeal. It's wallpaper paste. I'll help you roll the tables out, and then I have to check in."

"Thank you." He had his bag open and was laying out his tools. By the time I crossed the lab, he was taking caliper measurements on the skull.

"I'll be back to help when I can," I said. He nodded without taking his eyes off the skull.

I had patients as soon as I arrived at the ER. An early morning angler had hooked his thumb instead of a fish, and a tourist family had mistaken poison ivy for decorative plants. By the time I had them sewn and lotioned an orderly pushed in a gurney with Lou Tarnish strapped to it. Lou was a local farmer who cut up scrap metal for extra money. Unfortunately, he wasn't handy with his torch, and he had a tendency to set himself on fire. I had treated him twice before for burns.

"Again?" I asked.

Lou's wife, who had followed the gurney, answered for him. "This time the old fool sat on it, Doc." Mrs. Tarnish was a stocky woman clad in overalls and a plaid cotton shirt. Her hands, as they rubbed Lou's whiskery cheek, were callused and stained. A trickle of tobacco juice had escaped her mouth. I suspected that Lou and his wife had a lot in common.

I shoved a bed pan under Lou's chin. "I'm not doing anything until you get rid of your tobacco."

He extracted a brown mass from his mouth and placed it in the pan.

"Told you not to put that plug in, but no, you know everything," said Mrs. Tarnish, who used the pan to expel some of her juice. "You fix him up, Doc. I'm going to wait in the truck."

Lou had burned more overalls than skin, and I was able to treat him with antibiotics, ice, and some bandages. I gave him a doughnut cushion to sit on and admonished him to take his pills. He shuffled out to his wife, clutching his overalls around his waist.

It was afternoon before I rejoined Doctor Learner. He nodded a silent greeting.

"What did you learn today?" I asked, knowing that he was not likely to volunteer information.

"I believe I have determined the race of the first pair. The female was American Indian, at least in part, and the male was almost certainly black." He directed my attention to the skull of the first skeleton. "Note the wide nasal opening. This is characteristic of people of African descent. The nasal bone is also smooth where it joins the forehead, the brow ridges curve out a bit, and the eyes are wide-set. These traits, plus the color and texture of the hair that you so carefully saved, would confirm that the first skeleton belonged to a black man. Incidentally, he was right-handed and apparently involved in some activity that required predominate use of his right hand. His radius and humerus are both significantly longer than those of his left arm, which was caused by favored use. And he was shot. That chip on his third rib tested positive for lead. I suspect that the bullet you found caused his death."

I nodded, again fascinated. Doctor Learner moved to the female skeleton. "I'm afraid I can't determine this lady's cause of death, but given the circumstances, I doubt that it was natural." He flinched a smile, and I tried one back. His elbow banged his ribs. "Her teeth," he continued, "give the clue to her race. These shovel-shaped teeth are almost universal among Native Americans."

I squinted into the gaping mouth; the teeth did look like tiny shovels. "I'll be damned," I said.

"I also can't determine her handedness. I suspect that she was initially right-handed, but the injury reduced the use of that arm, and her left arm compensated. However, that's just a guess." His arm twitched. "That's about all I can tell you about the first pair. I'll perform Carbon Fourteen tests at the university lab to determine the age of the bones themselves. I am ready to begin with the next pair. Would you care to assist?"

Owen Learner and I spent the afternoon measuring bones, consulting his file charts, and examining teeth, ossification of joints, pelvic openings, skull fissures, and pits and cracks. By evening we knew that the two skeletons from the second room belonged to a white female and a black male, both in their late twenties or early thirties at the time of their deaths. Both were right-handed, and the male had several pronounced ridges on both femurs. Learner stated that these suggested that he had been a horseman. Stretching the legs over the horse and saddle, he explained, overly developed the adductor magus muscles, which left the ridges where they attached to the femurs. This was a common trait among Plains Indians. The bones of the female showed no abnormalities, and her pelvis had no scars from childbirth. Doctor Learner noted that she was missing several teeth, and her others were in poor shape. She had undoubtedly suffered from toothaches on more than one occasion. Her cause of death could not be determined, but a blow to the back of the head had killed the male. Doctor Learner found the fracture, but no signs of ossification, which meant that the body had made no attempt to heal the wound. Death is the only thing that prevents healing.

A thunderstorm greeted us as we exited. Doctor Learner

dashed to his car, trying to protect his bald head with his hands. I hurried to my van with water dripping from my face and hair. Light snaked across the sky, and the resulting implosion shook the van's windows. "Pretty close," I muttered, and wondered if I was safe in the van. Lightning was rare in Los Angeles; I wasn't accustomed to it. Another charge made its jagged way to earth, and the van's windows shook again. Rain pelted the roof, and the windshield resembled a waterfall. Driving would have to wait. After several minutes I saw the reflection of a strike flash like a camera as the storm moved behind me. The rain settled into a reasonable rhythm, and I guided the van homeward through flooded streets banked by flowing gutters.

Paul had fallen asleep on the couch. Work, I thought, will cut into your energy like nothing else. I woke him and steered him to the bedroom. He was snoring before I shut the door. I poured some brandy and listened to the last of the storm dribble off the roof. My son was in my house, and I felt content, a feeling so long absent I scarcely recognized it.

The rain broke the heat wave, and the pre-dawn air was chilly as I drove to work. Doctor Learner met me as I opened the morgue door. His dress was unvaried except for a subtle pattern of hexagons in today's red tie.

"I hope to finish here today," he announced without a greeting. "I should complete the Carbon Fourteen tests and any analysis you want for the material samples by early next week. You should have my complete report by the end of the week." His elbow banged his ribs. "I want to thank you for your assistance."

"My pleasure, Doctor. I'd like to help today if I can."

He nodded his agreement and began to lay out his tools. I knew the conversation was over, and I reported to the ER.

My cases were light: two sprained ankles resulting from their owners running to avoid last night's rain; I was back in the pathology lab before noon.

Doctor Learner looked up and stated, "I believe these final two skeletons were women, one white, and one black. With which skeleton was the fetus found?"

"Number five," I answered. "The one that was flat on the bed."

He nodded and patted the skull of the fifth skeleton. "She was white, I'm sure, and not too old. I'd say perhaps sixteen or seventeen." He picked up a femur. "There is still a small separation of the epiphyses and the shaft. The same condition exists on the clavicle. This usually disappears by eighteen." He replaced the femur and tilted the pelvis. "The pubic symphysis shows no ossification. She was certainly less than twenty, probably less than eighteen." He tilted the pelvis further. "This pregnancy, however, was not her first." I saw the groove in the preauricular sulcus, and nodded.

"It is very difficult to tell much about her fetus," Doctor Learner continued. "Sex characteristics are not present in fetal skeletons. All I can say is that it appeared well-formed and near term, at least seven months, otherwise, its fine bones would have completely deteriorated. The protection of the sealed room helped in their preservation, also. Of the last skeleton I only know sex and race. Would you care to assist?" he asked, fully cognizant of the answer.

By mid-afternoon the bones of the final skeleton revealed its owner to be tall, probably five ten, and judging from the weight of the bones and size of the clavicles, a hefty woman. Doctor Learner believed that she was the oldest of the six, past forty, and possibly fifty years old. She had borne children, probably several since the pelvic opening was especially wide. She was left-handed, and Doctor Learner pointed to fractures on her left hand that had not ossified.

"Either she was injured during her," he searched for the word, "final situation, or she fought hard against her abductors."

"I hope she fought," I said.

"So do I," he said with an uncharacteristic lack of objectivity.

I helped Learner pack his tools and charts into the trunk of his car. He had selected a bone from each skeleton and samples of the fabrics that clung to some of the bones. He afforded me a final handshake with his tapered fingers and promised me return of the bones with his final report. He looked at me through his rimless glasses and said, "A challenge. A young man needs a challenge."

***

Since Paul would be working late tending bar, I ate in the hospital cafeteria and drove to Bird's house to give him a preliminary report. Bird was on his front porch watching his two daughters chase lightning bugs in the waning light. I joined him and told him what I knew.

"So what we have is four women of various races and ages, two black men in their thirties, one of whom may have ridden a horse. One man was shot, the other clubbed, one woman may have tried to defend herself, and another had bad teeth. That's not a whole lot to go on."

"No," I admitted. "But Doctor Learner is going to perform more tests. He said he'd have the complete results by the end of next week."

"So I guess we wait a little longer. At least the media has

cooled their interest a bit." Bird stretched his legs over the porch rail. "I see Paul is working at the Inn at the Pines Lodge."

"Yeah, in fact, he's there now. How'd you know that?"

"I'm the sheriff, and I know stuff. He going to stay awhile?"

"I think so," I said and told Bird the details of the arrangement for the car and our conversation with Maria.

Bird slapped his knee. "Damn, boy, you're hot. First you mow down that Christen fellow, and now Maria. I like it."

"Well, it hasn't all worked out yet, and Paul deserves most of the credit for Maria."

"Better than it was," said Bird. "How's Paul adjusting?"

I rolled my cigar for a minute. "I think all right. He's willing to work, and he seems kind of relieved to be away from Maria."

"Boy's not stupid," said Bird and pointed his bony finger at me. "Don't you stick your head up your ass. Talk to the boy."

I nodded, stung by his directness, but realized it was well-intended.

"Bird," Patty called from the screen door. "Call the girls for their baths. Oh, Bill, I didn't know you were here. Want some lemonade?"

"No thanks, Patty. I'm going home in a minute. I'm going to Des Moines tomorrow to pick up Paul's car. You want anything?"

"Don't think so," said Bird. He tossed his head toward Patty. "Unless you come across one of those hot-blooded women I've been hearing about."

Patty reached out the door and slapped him on the top of his head. "I've got all the hot blood you need. Now, call the girls."

Bird called his daughters from where they ran among the

shadows of the yew trees that formed his property boundary. He examined their cache of bugs flashing in a Mason jar, roughly squeezed and patted each girl and ushered them through the front door to their mother. He returned to his seat, draped his legs over the porch rail and announced, "Bill, my boy, this is the place to live life."

I grunted noncommittally.

"I'm serious," he continued. "Look out there." He gestured into the darkness. "Kids can safely play after dark. Nobody's getting car-jacked. Nobody's selling drugs. Anybody can walk down the streets. Not like in Los Angeles where you got pimps, pushers, and prostitutes up and down every main street, and a bunch of non-Americans driving around shooting everyone with machines guns. Don't know how you could live in that cesspool."

"We had other things, too. Theaters, concerts, movie studios, pro sports teams, the ocean, Disneyland." I vaguely wondered if there was a connection between the prurient and the sublime.

"Yeah, there's that, but it's fading fast. Mostly there're wild, mean streets and scared citizens. But not here," he said proudly. "We work damned hard to keep it that way, too."

"Well, I don't know," I wheedled. "You got that whorehouse out by the amusement park. That's not all that wholesome."

"That's different," Bird snapped. "Man needs an outlet once in a while. But you don't ever see those girls hustling on the street. They got no pimps to beat them up; they better not be messing with any drugs, and when they come in town they better act proper. If not, their butts get bounced faster than a basketball at a tournament.

"I've never been to Los Angeles, but I've seen pictures.

Buildings, walls, and signs so covered with graffiti you can't tell what they are. Gangsters going around shooting up cars and houses. Half-naked hookers hanging around in the streets. And in the middle of all that you got little kids trying to play. You can't tell me that's good."

"No," I agreed. "It's not good."

"Tell you what else isn't good. You got all them minorities out there, and each one wants special treatment. Get all kinds of favoritism just because one of their ancestors might have had a hard go. One group gets something, then all the others want it, too. You know who pays for that. Us regular Americans who built this country, that's who. We didn't whine about it and expect a handout when it got tough, either. Not like these prima donnas that want to suck everything out of the country."

"That's quite a speech, Bird," I said.

He laughed. "I guess I got carried away. And I guess I'm proud of Bishop and the part I play to keep it safe and sound. All this business with the skeletons kind of shook me up. Be glad when things are normal again."

"Yeah, me, too."

"Well," he punched at my shoulder, "I better get in and help the girls get settled for bed or Patty will give me hell for not properly sharing in the nurturing of our offspring." He laughed again. "Read that shit in some magazine. See you later."

CHAPTER ELEVEN

Paul had worked late and dozed most of the way to Des Moines. He watched as I thumped fenders and doors, pulled the tie rods, listened to the motors, shifted gears, and bounced the springs of the two junk yard cars. I encouraged Paul to choose the 1972 Comet largely because it had little rust and a six cylinder motor with a standard transmission which would be easier to work on. We returned to Bishop with it strapped to Johnny's car hauler. Paul dozed again, and I watched the corn tassels undulate in the breeze and fiddled with the radio to stay awake.

We shoved the Comet into the garage next to my Mercury, and I told Paul that tomorrow we'd start stripping it to see what parts needed to be replaced. Paul's nap revitalized him, and he asked about Bishop's nighttime entertainment.

"Well, it's a short list," I said. "Got a movie house off the square, but it won't be showing a first run movie. Could shoot some pool at the Golden Eagle. Community center has Bingo and square dancing lessons. Then, of course, you can hang out at the Dairy Queen and watch the shad flies electrocute themselves in the bug lights. We live pretty high in Bishop."

"Yeah, I can see. I was thinking of somewhere I could take a girl."

"Whoa. Been in town a week and already got a date. I guess those local girls were dazzled by your big city ways. Who's the girl?"

"Cindy Schmidt. She's a maid at the lodge this summer. She's in teacher training at the University of Northern Iowa. You know her?"

"No, but unless she got hurt or sick, I probably wouldn't," I said. "This may be a little corny, but you might try the early movie and on Saturdays at ten o'clock there's a fireworks show at the amusement park. It's kind of pretty. After that, you're on your own."

"Sounds pretty good." Paul started towards the house, stopped, and asked, "What are you going to do, Dad?"

"Thought I might get this car jacked up, and I got a new book I started."

Paul poked at a clump of water grass with his toe. "Do you ever date, Dad?"

I studied the end of my cigar. "I guess not very much. I don't suppose having coffee with my ER nurse counts. I'm not very good at that kind of stuff."

"You should get out more," he said. This time his eyes weren't dancing.

***

My father had left behind a small life insurance policy, a two-bedroom house, and a garage full of mechanic's tools. It was the latter for which I was the most grateful. After years of trying to repair cars with a screwdriver and a crescent wrench, I finally had access to the proper tools. Paul and I used those tools to remove parts from his Comet. I suggested that the machine shop rebuild the carburetor, perform a valve job, and turn the brake drums. I planned to order new brake linings, wheel cylinders, shocks, hoses, and a battery. By late afternoon parts covered the garage floor, and Paul and I were embedded with grease and grime.

"This is hard work. We really going to save money?"

"Shit, yeah," I said as I began to sort the parts into boxes. "We should have that car running like new for about five hundred dollars. A mechanic might charge as much as two grand."

"Jeez, that is good. Where'd you learn to do this Dad? Granddad teach you?"

"Most of it. Some I learned working on the Mercury."

"How'd you get that Mercury, anyway?"

I straightened and stretched my back. "That, my boy, is the first car I bought in California. I got it cheap from a guy whose father had owned it; his father had died, and he wanted to get rid of it. The old guy didn't drive it much; only put forty thousand miles on it in fifteen years. It was made in the Ford plant in San Pedro, but that's gone now. Never was out of California until I shipped it here. That car got me through college and med school. Took your mother to the hospital in it to have you. When I started working, I decided to fix it up. I've been doing a little at a time for years. May get it finished some day, but it really doesn't matter. Car's just part of me now. Besides," I added, "your mother hated it. Refused to drive it. After our divorce it was the only possession she left me."

Paul smiled, "Lot I don't know about you, Dad."

"Yeah, but it's never too late to learn. Come on. We'd better clean up and get some dinner."

***

I spent the next week working in the ER, repairing Paul's car, and waiting for Doctor Learner's report. It arrived at Bird's office Friday morning, and he brought it to me.

"I skimmed it a bit, but there's a bunch of medical terms. Figured you better see it."

Learner had prepared a report of several pages for each skeleton specifying damaged bones, exact measurements, and delineating methods and tests applied. I had expected nothing less. I thumbed through it to find the results of the Carbon-14 tests.

"Bird, did you read this part?"

Bird was settling on an examination table. "Probably not. What does it say?"

"That each skeleton without exception is approximately sixty years old."

Bird bolted up and grabbed the report. "Where?" he demanded, read, and mouthed the words, "Sixty years. That means," he said, "that each person was killed sixty years ago, around nineteen thirty?"

"That's exactly what it means," I said.

"They were in that hotel all that time? When my granddad stayed there?"

"I assume so. The bones were too naturally placed to have been moved there."

Bird tossed the report on the table. "Ain't that a pisser. Everyone all wrapped up in something that happened sixty years ago." He flapped his arms a couple of times.

I retrieved the report and read further. "It looks like those trace fibers are consistent with that," I said. "Those fragments that were stuck to the bones were all cotton except one that was silk. No nylon, which came after the war. No rayon. No polyester. The buttons were bone, shell, and metal. No plastic. I'd say they were there for sixty years."

Bird slapped his hands. "Well, I suspect that will end it then, thank God."

"What? Why?"

"How's anybody going to investigate something that happened that long ago? Any witnesses are probably dead. Nobody can even identify the victims. No clues to follow up. I don't think the media's going to be very interested now."

"I guess," I said.

Bird gathered up the report. "I'm going to show it to the mayor, and let him decide how to handle it, but I'll bet it's done." He strode toward the door and turned. "I guess I was wrong about Nate Griswold."

Bird might have been wrong about Nate Griswold, but he was right about the matter being dead. The next day the mayor announced the age of the skeletons at a news conference and informed his audience that the case would remain open and the sheriff's office would use any information offered from the public, but the investigation would not be active. Bird echoed the mayor and stated that too many years had passed to determine anything about the crime, victims, or the perpetrators.

The media also met Bird's prediction. Aside from a few on-the-street interviews for local color, their broadcasts of the news conference ended their interest in the skeletons. As the humidity and heat of July continued into August, the lead stories and headlines pondered the fate of the corn crop. The county council approved the request to continue the demolition of the hotel, and I bagged and stored the skeletons in the morgue. Bishop had had its moment of attention; the normality of hazy heat, droning ski boats, and the cacophony of insects returned.

***

When the evenings dropped the temperature a few degrees, I reassembled Paul's car. Sometimes Paul helped me, but often he tended bar or dated Cindy. I preferred his assistance, but didn't demand it and was genuinely pleased that he was responsible in his work and had adapted to Bishop.

Maria, to my surprise, sent all the paper work for the BMW with her signatures in the appropriate places. She included a short note to Paul in which she managed to wish him luck; I, of course, was not acknowledged. In what I knew was her attempt at the last word, she sent everything postage due, but Paul and I were able to deliver the BMW to auction. We tried every accessory as the smooth leather seats and suspension negated the tar-filled cracks on the highway to Sioux City. We returned by bus, which had no accessories and did not feature smooth leather seats.

CHAPTER TWELVE

By mid-August with shorter days, fewer lightning bugs, and conversations concerning corn rather than skeletons, the demolition crew finished its work at the old hotel. A few errant bricks and a thick coating of dust on the surrounding plants were all that remained of the building that had grandly striven to be the Tourist Center of the Midwest, but degenerated into a forlorn eyesore and the temporary grave for seven beings.

From time to time, when it was slow in the ER, I walked to the morgue and looked at the body bags that held the bones of those beings. Bird, the mayor, and the rest of Bishop were satisfied that their mystery had been solved. For some reason I was disturbed by their resting in limbo in the morgue. I found myself creating scenarios that could have led the six people to their deaths in the hotel. I certainly didn't admit this to anyone, and I wasn't sure why I did it.

On an August evening, while Paul and I were sitting on the porch enjoying the cooler air, he informed me of his intention to follow Cindy to the University of Northern Iowa at the start of the fall semester. Once there he planned to find employment and an apartment and possibly return to college classes by the spring semester.

"I take it then," I said, "that you and Cindy get along pretty well." I removed my feet from the porch rail and faced him.

"Oh, yeah. Great. Best thing that happened to me was coming to Bishop and meeting her."

"This is love, then?"

Paul nodded; his eyes shone in the dusk.

"You and Cindy going to be sharing this apartment?" I asked.

Paul nodded again. "That's the plan."

"Planning marriage?"

"We're going to wait until we finish school and start our careers."

"I see. Cindy pregnant?"

"Dad, jeez ..."

"Hey, I'm a doctor, and I know how stuff works. Is she?"

"No, of course not."

"How can you be so sure?"

"Because we always used ..." he stopped.

"A rubber, condom, prophylactic," I finished.

I could see Paul redden in the shadows. He nodded.

"Good. I'm glad you're having safe sex. And stop being embarrassed. Sex is normal. You just have to respect its consequences. What do Cindy's parents think about all this?"

"They seem to like me okay," Paul said. "She's telling them now. I don't see much of a problem. We're both twenty-two."

"Paul, you must understand that no matter how old Cindy is, she will always be Mr. Schmidt's little girl, just like you'll always be my little boy." I sipped some brandy. "I suspect that we'll be hearing from Mr. Schmidt before the evening is over."

"You going to be on my side, Dad?"

"This what you really want?"

He nodded.

"Then I'm on your side."

Within the hour Mr. Schmidt did indeed call and made diplomatic inquiries about Paul and myself. I made the same inquiries, perhaps not as diplomatically, we expressed mutual concern, and I reluctantly agreed to a get-acquainted dinner on Sunday.

***

The Schmidts farmed a sizable spread in the valley south of town not far from where Granddad Mullins established his homestead almost a century ago. From the appearance of their home, out buildings, and new Oldsmobile in the drive, the Schmidts operated at a profit.

Mr. Schmidt, who was approaching the Comet before Paul had it parked, was the size of an oak tree. He had a square face permanently reddened by years in the sun, and his white hair bounced with every step. I felt as if I were trapped at a railroad crossing with a locomotive bearing down. I managed to extricate myself from the car before the locomotive collided into me with an iron handshake and a pile-driver thump on my back. He introduced himself as Casper Schmidt and then collided with Paul. He coupled the two of us under his arms and guided us to the house under full steam. Paul was able to free himself to greet Cindy in the living room, but, unfortunately, I had no one to greet, and Mr. Schmidt continued to guide me into his study and deposited me in a chair across from his desk. The wall behind the desk was covered with the heads of animals, enough to start a small zoo. The opposite wall held guns of every description. Mr. Schmidt sat behind his desk and reduced his steam level by fingering a letter opener that had a handle made of a large fang.

Mr. Schmidt, I concluded, was an asshole.

"Not sure where to begin here, Doctor," he said. "It is 'Doctor,' isn't it?"

I assured him that it was, but he could call me Bill.

"Well, call me Cap. Everyone does. I don't really know much about you or your family, Bill."

"I could say the same thing to you, Cap."

His eyes snapped from the fanged letter opener and looked into mine. "My family was one of the first to settle in this area," he said, confused. He clearly hadn't expected to defend his family to me.

"So was mine," I said. "In fact, our grandfathers were neighbors."

"Really?"

"Our farm was about a half mile to the east. I think it's owned by a corporation now."

His white hair bounced as his head shot toward me. "Those goddamn corporations and businessmen are just ruining farming for everyone." He smashed his desk top with his pile-driver fist. "But that's not what I need to talk about now, and this sure isn't going like I planned."

He let off more steam and settled into his chair. "Cindy is my only child."

"Paul is my only one."

Mr. Schmidt lost the rest of his steam and rested his head in his hand. He looked human and vulnerable. "Guess we're both in the same boat, then."

"Looks like."

"How do you feel about it?"

"Scared shitless."

Mr. Schmidt raised his eyes. His face displayed age and worry lines. "Boy, you know it. Haven't slept right since Cindy told us. What do you think we should do?"

"As much as I'd like to ground Paul and send him to his room, I can't. And you can't treat Cindy like that anymore, either. Whether we think so or not, they are adults, and I guess we better hope they act like adults and are as smart as we think they are."

"I know you're right. Mildred ... Hell, you haven't even met my wife. This has gotten me all turned around. Anyway, Mildred, she said the same thing. Wish I *could* ground her, though. She's just too young to be doing this. Well, not really, but I always think of her ..." he stopped and rubbed his eye.

"As your little girl," I finished. "And Paul's my little boy."

We smiled at each other and both rubbed our eyes.

Mildred, who, though by no means as large as her husband, had amply spread into middle age and possessed two readily apparent qualities. She was a skilled engineer for her locomotive and guided her husband into a jovial host. Second, she was a superb cook who believed in substantial portions. Since I usually subsisted on deli sandwiches and canned soup, I thoroughly enjoyed each of my three helpings of smoked ham, sweet potatoes, and creamed beans. This seemed to embarrass Paul, but delighted Mildred, and she promised me the leftovers for sandwiches. Mr. Schmidt, or Cap as I had begun to call him, had a collection of antique plows housed in a shed next to his barn. Most had belonged to his ancestors, and he related a story about each one while we sipped brandy. By the time Paul and I left I decided that Cap wasn't quite the asshole that I thought, but I was relieved for Paul's sake that Cindy seemed to take after her mother.

"What did you and Mr. Schmidt talk about all that time?" Paul asked as we turned onto Main Street.

"Little boys and little girls, and finally a lot about plows," I said.

"He's really a nice guy. He just comes on a little strong."

"I noticed," I said and yawned, trying to get comfortable on the Comet's bench seat.

"Oh, Dad, I forgot to ask you. Next Friday the lodge is having a dance to end the summer season. There's going to be a live band, and they expect a big crowd. I'm going to tend one of the bars. Anyway, it's going to have a 'fifties theme, and Mr. Jason wanted to know if you would park your Mercury by the entrance. You know, to kind of set the mood."

"I suppose. It'll be in a safe place?"

"Oh, yeah. It'll be right in front by the valet guys. He said you'd get a free admission to the dance."

"Okay, I'll get it cleaned up this week. You can take it when you go to work Friday."

"I thought you'd drive it to the dance," said Paul.

"I'm usually pretty beat on Fridays, and I don't dance very well."

"One night wouldn't hurt. Get out and have a little fun. You might get to like it."

I yawned. "You got the car. I'll think about the dance."

***

The dance, as I saw in advertisements in almost every business window, was billed as the social event of the summer, and it seemed the entire town planned to attend. Even Emma informed me that if I wanted a sandwich on Friday I had to order early. She was planning to "cut a rug." Paul persisted in reminding me that

I would have a good time, and I finally agreed to go, mostly so that he would talk about something else.

The Inn at the Pines Lodge had indeed planned an event. Torches burned on the perimeter of the grounds; several cooks labored over barbecue grills on the lodge's south lawn. A bandstand of plywood and two-by-fours supported massive speakers and a jumble of cords. Bleachers had been erected on the lake front to provide a view of the fireworks show. The ballroom contained a proliferation of cocktail tables and three bars, one of which was tended by Paul.

"Did you bring the car?" asked Paul, when I ordered a drink from him.

"Yeah. Mr. Jason had me park it by the entrance to the drive. Looks pretty good there."

"Great. Cindy and her parents are outside someplace. I'll try to get away when it's not so busy."

I wasn't in any great hurry to encounter Cap Schmidt, and I wandered around clusters of poodle skirts sported mostly by girls born well after the 'fifties. Boys, combing their newly-found ducktails and rolling cigarette packs into the sleeves of their T-shirts, watched the girls from the perimeter of the lawn. Only the costumes change, I thought, as I made my way to the bleachers and empty space.

"Shit bricks. I never expected to see you here." Bird rounded the opposite side of the bleachers. "I was just checking on the fireworks. An elected man's work is never done," he said with mock seriousness. "Come on. Patty and I got a table under that shade tree." He pointed and strode off.

I figured I'd enjoy Bird's company more than the Schmidts', and I trotted a bit to catch up.

"What got you out of the house?" Bird asked as we sat down.

"Paul wanted me to bring the Mercury. It's out front."

"Yeah? We'll have to check it out later. Bill has a helluva car," Bird said to the other couple at the table. "Say, Bill, you remember Larry and Karen Reisling? They were a year behind us in school. Her name was Keonig then."

We nodded at each other, but I didn't remember them. I listened while the four reminisced about high school. Bird would occasionally draw me into the conversation, but mostly I sipped my drink and felt out of place.

At dusk, the torch lights became noticeable, and the band mounted the stage and opened with a rendition of Billy Haley's "Rock Around the Clock" followed by Buddy Holly's "Peggy Sue." They moved into Chuck Berry and Elvis, and Bird and Larry escorted their wives to the twirling skirts and jumping saddle shoes on the dance floor. Feeling more out of place, I wandered with my intended objective being a second drink. Paul called to me as soon as I entered the ballroom and waved for me to join the Schmidts and himself at a cocktail table.

I inwardly winced, but maintained suitable social skills while I conversed with Paul and the Schmidts. Mildred and Cindy were dressed in identical skirts and matador blouses. Cindy was a younger, slimmer version of her mother with her blond hair pulled into a pony tail. When Paul led Cindy to the dance floor, I considered Mildred's ample figure and wondered if Cindy would have a similar fate, and then wondered what it mattered. After the dance, Paul returned to his bar, and I felt that I had met my social obligations and excused myself. I got my second drink from Paul and told him I'd be going soon.

"Wait, Dad. I want you to meet someone," Paul said, and guided me to the end of the bar where a lady in a business suit was sipping orange juice and drumming her red nails against the glass.

"Mrs. Harden," Paul said, "I'd like you to meet my father, Doctor Mullins."

Mrs. Harden extended her red nails. "My pleasure."

"She's the one who organized this whole thing," Paul added and returned to mixing drinks.

"I'm impressed," I said. "Real nice set up and crowd. Even I had fun. Must have been a big job."

She sipped her juice and nodded. "And I'm beat and would like to go home, but my car's in the shop, and I can't get a ride until this is over."

"If you just need a ride, I'll take you home. That is, if your husband won't mind."

"He won't. I'm a widow."

"I'm sorry. I didn't mean ..." I didn't know how to finish, and I mentally rebuffed myself for saying the wrong thing as quickly as possible. To my relief, Mrs. Harden smiled and patted my hand.

"It's all right. You didn't hurt a thing. But I do live quite a ways out."

"That's fine. I need to drive the car some anyway."

She finished her juice, put her hand on my arm, and said, "Since you're taking me home, you should call me Emily."

I liked her hand. "Bill," I said and smiled.

At the entrance to the lodge she pointed to my car. "Isn't that a lovely car that Mr. Jason got? It really added to the atmosphere."

"I like it," I said and walked her to it.

"You can't do that," she blurted as I opened the passenger door for her.

"Do what?" I asked, frantically wondering what social blunder I had committed now.

"You're not supposed to touch the car. What if the owner saw you?"

"Emily, I am the owner. It's my car." I held up the keys as a form of proof.

Emily stared at both me and the keys for a moment, then collapsed laughing on my chest. "You just didn't look the type. Oh, I'm so tired I don't know what I'm saying." She climbed into the seat. "Let's go," she said.

I started the Mercury and guided it down the drive and wondered how I could get Emily's head back on my chest.

"Drive north around the lake and take a left at the junction of one forty-two. It's about fifteen miles out," she directed. "Is it all right if I take off my shoes? My feet are killing me."

"Sure," I agreed, and Emily adjusted herself to a sideways position and was breathing rhythmically before I had driven past the lake. The turn onto route 142 caused her to shift and her head rested on my shoulder. It wasn't my chest, but I still liked it. Her hair smelled like lilacs, and her curled form easily fit on the Mercury's front seat. She was snoring lightly after I had traveled about fifteen miles, and not wanting to wake her or move her head, I slowed to inspect names on mailboxes. The fifth one read "Harden," and I turned up a drive lined with hedge roses to a ranch-style brick home and parked by the double garage. A German shepherd began to circle the car and convinced me that the most prudent move at this point would be to wake Emily.

"Emily, you're home," I said and patted her shoulder.

Her head abruptly left my shoulder, and she sat blinking and glancing at me, the car, and her garage door. When she recognized her home and remembered me, she sank back in the seat. "I fell asleep. God, I was so tired. I'm sorry."

"Don't be. I'm sorry I had to wake you, but your dog seems a bit disturbed by my presence."

"Oh, that's Pansy," Emily said as she replaced her shoes.

"Pansy?"

"Yeah. That gives you an idea of how tough she is. Just looking for a handout and a back rub." Emily exited the car and walked to my window, patting the shepherd's head. "Thanks for the ride. It must be a good car; I never felt a bump. I'd ask you in for a drink, but I'd just fall asleep again. Why don't you call me at the lodge someday next week. I'm better company when I'm awake."

"Okay, I will," I said, and then blurted, "I had a really nice time tonight." I was sure that I had reverted to a pimply adolescent on his first date.

Emily didn't seem to notice. "I'm glad, Bill. Thanks again for the ride. Goodnight." She patted my arm and walked to her house with Pansy at her heels.

As I drove to Bishop I did feel like that pimply-faced adolescent who'd just had his first serious date. The air was fresher, the car ran smoother, and I indulged in an urge to sing along with the radio. The dance at the lodge was still going when I passed, but I felt too good to be around people. I drove through the streets of Bishop singing with the radio before sitting on my porch sipping brandy and listening to the last of the cicadas. I knew Emily accounted for my good feelings, although there was no logical reason that she should. I had spent less than an hour with her, during most of which she slept. Nonetheless, I liked her and wanted to see her again.

Paul arrived home in the early morning. "Jeez, Dad. Thought you'd be in bed. You okay?"

"Just relaxing. Dance finish up all right?"

"Yeah. Big turn out. Got a lot of tips."

I pulled the cigar out of my mouth. "Do you know Mrs. Harden very well?" I asked.

"She runs the catering office and books the events where I tend bar. I work with her pretty often. Nice lady."

"Yeah. She asked me to call her next week. Think she meant it?"

"Probably. And I think you should do it."

"What if she just said it to be nice because I took her home?"

"Then I guess she'll start vicious rumors and have you run out of town. Come on, Dad. If she said to call her then call her and stop sweating it. I'm going to bed. Oh, listen. Cindy and I are taking Tuesday and Wednesday off next week to go to Cedar Falls to get an apartment. That all right?"

"Yeah. Good idea. Beat the rush when school starts."

"That's what we thought. Think the Comet will make it?"

"Should make it to New York. If you have trouble, I'll come get you."

"Okay. Good night. And call her, Dad."

I waved at him and listened to the cicadas perform their last chorus.

Late Summer, 1931

1

The train whistle woke him before dawn; he lay on his damp sheets looking at the gray rectangle formed by the room's single window. The window was open as far as possible, but its thin curtain hung motionless. The night had dropped the temperature a few degrees, but the still air kept the room uncomfortably warm, and sweat clung to his body. The whistle was followed by the scraping and squealing of metal wheels against the tracks as the engineer slowed the train for the curve that preceded the switching station. The train, he knew, was the early freight from Omaha, and it would be switched at Bishop to either Minneapolis or Chicago.

Noah Atherton hated the sounds of the whistle and screeching wheels, not because they awakened him, but because he knew that when the train slowed the vermin jumped off to join the other vermin camped in the woods by the tracks. Their numbers had increased dramatically in the past year, and, at times, there were well over a hundred sheltered in canvas tents, bedrolls, or simply by tree branches. Before Noah's father died he had explained about the depressed economy, which, he said, was caused by over-speculation on the stock market and resulted in high unemployment.

Noah, who recognized his father's wisdom, understood little of his explanations and simply recognized, as his father did, that the vermin threatened him, his family, and his town, and that he hated them. As he lay sweating on the sheets he could imagine their sordid lives in the boxcars and tents. Debaucheries, he knew. Drinking, gambling, thievery, and, his throat tightened, sex. He had seen women both on the trains and in the camp, and he knew no respectable woman would live like that. They were whores, he was certain, and regularly committed all types of sins.

Noah felt his sweat turn cold in the warm room and felt his penis tingle. He tried to shift his mind from those thoughts, but the visions of their sins were too vivid to ignore and played across his mind like the pictures in the Nickelodeon in the hardware store. Images of naked breasts, buttocks, and, although he knew it was the worst, vaginas, flashed in his mind. Despite his efforts to stop, those images yielded to more lurid ones: a woman fondling an erect penis, licking it, and finally placing it into her vagina. By now he had lost all control, and he gripped his rigid member under his shorts. Images kept flickering as he stroked faster and gripped tighter until he came to the image that so repulsed and thrilled him that his stroking became frenzied: a black man with a huge black dick like a bull, shoving it into a white woman. When the black man turned the woman over and entered her from behind, Noah soaked his shorts.

He panted in the pre-dawn light, the sheets now wet with sweat, and guilt replaced the lurid images. He removed his shorts and wiped himself with the end of the sheet. He fell on his knees and prayed for forgiveness and that his mother wouldn't find out.

Noah knew his father had been wise, even if Noah didn't always understand him, but he worshipped and feared his mother. From his mother he had learned right from wrong by the sting of a switch on his buttocks and legs, and he feared her wrath if she caught him masturbating again. Although the last whipping had hurt terribly, it also set his penis tingling. This confused Noah, and he wondered if his mother's whippings had lost their usefulness for him. He thought it must be because he was now grown up, which, being two weeks shy of his twentieth birthday, he was.

His mother also taught him to preach and to hate. The preaching came from countless hours of her reading the Bible to him and from her putting him on the stage in a revival tent when he was ten years old. Mixed with his mother's Bible instruction came the idea that the white race was God's chosen people and all others were pitiful rejects given to animalistic existences. As Noah approached puberty, white women who were not pure of body were also included in the pitiful rejects. By the time he was in high school he had honed his preaching skills to the point that he could enthrall a tent full of revivalists on a hot summer's night, and he had become his father's assistant in the operation of Bishop's Ku Klux Klan.

His father had been a member of the Klan since marrying his mother, a proper Southern Lady. His father had done his best to spread the Klan's words of truth through Bishop, but he had approached the task from an intellectual standpoint, as he did most tasks, and few people understood his appeals. When he died the previous year, Noah had taken command of the few members and begun to preach to them with the fire that he used in revival tents. The membership grew, and the weekly meetings at the Atherton farm were marked by at least a score of men, a burning cross, and Noah's impassioned voice heralding the superiority of the white race.

Meetings, as Noah instinctively knew, were only successful if they attained a goal. Some weeks before Noah had decided on a goal, and tonight, he thought, with the right preaching and with a little of the corn whiskey that his friend Joe Corneilson made, he was certain his goal would be realized. The camp of vermin would be eradicated, and his power would be cemented in Bishop.

The thought of that power and the vermin writhing in torment made his loins twitch again. He prayed to remove the feeling, poured water into the wash basin on his dresser, soaked his face in it, and dressed for chores in the gray light.

2

Joe Corneilson stood on the bed of the truck sweating under his sheet and hood. The several torches next to the truck stank of kerosene, and their heat made him more uncomfortable, but he was happy. For the first time in his twenty-three years he felt important. Noah Atherton had chosen him to be his assistant, and he alone was standing with him on the truck bed. A group of perhaps three dozen men in sheets and hoods clustered around the truck and were listening intently to Noah.

Joe was not listening to Noah's exhortations. Noah had told him earlier that afternoon that they would burn out the camp tonight, and then entrusted him with two tasks: first, to provide an adequate supply of whiskey, and second, and by far the more important, to lead a group of men and direct the burning. Joe had never been in charge of anything, and he was nervous. Noah was the only person, besides his mother, who had shown any belief in him. He fiercely wanted to please Noah, and when Noah whipped off his hood and raised his hands with a triumphant cheer, he did the same. He knew that this signaled the end of Noah's preaching, and he hopped off the bed and retrieved four jugs of whiskey from the cab. He passed these among the men, and in a few minutes he heard someone shout, "Joe makes the best whiskey in Iowa," followed by a cheer from the rest of the men. Joe felt his face flush, and his chest ached with pride.

Before all the whiskey could be consumed, Noah grabbed one of the torches and directed some of the men to board the truck and the others to a hay wagon hitched to a team of. horses. Joe was to drive the truck to the road next to the railroad tracks above the camp and wait for Noah's signal. Noah would be approaching from the opposite side, and, as he had explained that afternoon, the vermin would be trapped between them.

As he drove the truck down the rutted lane away from the Atherton farm, anxiety replaced Joe's feeling of pride. Without Noah to give him confidence, he questioned if he could manage his group of men. He also wondered if it was right to burn and destroy the few belongings those people had. Noah called them vermin and said they were evil, but Joe thought that they might just be poor. He knew both he and his mother were not far from a similar plight. Since his father died, Joe had been unable to get enough crops planted to pay the mortgage, and his mother had received several letters from the bank.

Joe guided the truck behind a tree by the road, reached for the whiskey jug on the floor of the cab, and took a long drink. He heard the men getting restless behind him, and he took another drink. The whiskey burned his stomach and gave him the nerve to guide the men to a clump of bushes across the road. There he told them to have their torches ready for lighting and to listen for Noah's signal. To Joe's relief the men complied and silently waited, passing the jug among them.

Joe became anxious within a few minutes and thought that Noah might not appear. He told himself to relax, that the hay wagon couldn't move as fast as the truck, but he still felt doubts. He had just taken a hasty pull from the jug when he heard Noah's hoot owl signal and saw the torches on the other side of the camp. He struck a match, lit his torch, and passed it to light the others. He jammed the hood over his head and with a whoop, charged through the bushes surrounding the camp. The men followed him, and he could see the men that Noah led, and he relaxed. He stopped in the center of the camp and viewed the chaos around him through his hooded mask. The scattering residents reminded him of field mice scampering before a plow. Maybe they were vermin after all.

Joe saw some men pulling down a tent, and he directed them to bring it to the center. He grabbed some boxes and paper and quickly got a fire started. The men intuitively understood and threw tents, clothes, suitcases, and bedrolls onto the fire until it blazed almost to the tops of the trees. Its heat drenched Joe with sweat, but he was oblivious and continued feeding the fire, happy to belong.

When the fire had consumed every flammable article in the camp and had begun to die, Noah appeared and with the flames dancing in his eyes said, "Get a couple of men and wait until daybreak to see if anyone comes back. Then drive the highway to Bishop to get any vermin there. I already have three on the back of the wagon. Get some more, and we'll have fun." He stepped closer and slipped Joe a small revolver. "Take care of any problems with that." Joe nodded, his eyes glued to the flames in Noah's eyes. He was smiling under his hood. No one had trusted him with a gun before.

3

The whistle and the train's slowing woke John Peterson, and he clutched his satchel to him and peered into the dark boxcar. He listened over the screeching wheels for any sounds of movement within the car, and satisfied he was still alone, relaxed. John hated traveling by freights, what with railroad bulls and thieving hobos after what little he had left, but he could afford no other means. A few months before he had ridden herd over a sizable number of cattle in West Texas, as he had for the ten previous years. During the last few years the land had grown drier and was able to support fewer and fewer cattle. The owner sold off the cattle he couldn't support and laid off hands. John stayed until the last year when the land became so brittle that it could hardly support a jack rabbit. The owner had given John a handshake and thirty dollars for his horse and suggested that he try to get work at the stockyards up North.

John hid a ten dollar bill in the heel of each boot and rode a freight to Kansas City. He rode another to Omaha, but found no work at either place. In a hobo camp by the Missouri River he considered his options. Some time ago he had written a childhood friend about the impending failure of the ranch, and his friend had invited him to stay with him and his new wife on their farm near Bishop, Iowa. John had kept the letter, and he felt it in his jacket pocket. He didn't want to impose on his friend; he was likely having as hard a time as everyone else, but he hadn't found any work. Besides, John thought, it was on the way to Chicago, and his luck might be better there. While he waited for an east-bound freight, an old hobo with a white beard that covered his chest, told him that Bishop had a big camp and was a good place to get some grub and spread a bedroll. John felt that going to Bishop was the best decision he could make. He caught a freight as it slowed for the Missouri bridge, and pleased that he had selected an empty car, had settled into sleep.

It was still dark when he hopped to the ground; he picked his way off the graveled rail path to a tree. He leaned against it to wait for the light to show him the way to the camp. The acrid smell of smoke burned his nose, and he wondered who would have a fire that early in the morning.

Dawn revealed a well-used path leading down an embankment and into a clump of trees. He followed it, hoping for some coffee. That hope vanished when he saw the source of the smoke. Smoldering canvas, blankets, and boxes marked the remains of a bonfire in what had been the center of the camp. Cans, cooking utensils, and scraps of clothing were scattered throughout the wooded area. John clutched his satchel tighter and turned to leave when he heard a voice say, "Nigger, you weren't very smart coming back here." He turned to the voice, saw it belonged to a man perched on the back of a flatbed truck, and opened his mouth to explain that he hadn't "come back." He saw the man smile a toothless grin and raise a rifle, and he knew any explanations would be futile.

4

Edna Davidson sat in the shade of the bus shelter at the edge of Bishop. She had disembarked from the Perry bus, and was searching in her handbag for the map with the directions to the farm where she hoped to find work as a cook and housekeeper. Edna was a large woman in her late forties who moved slowly, and she wasn't looking forward to the walk of several miles to the farmhouse that the map suggested. She produced a thin scarf from her pocket and tied up her gray hair to protect it from the dust from the road. She needed the job badly and wanted to look her best when she arrived. For the past month she had lived with her sister and her husband in Perry, but they were struggling with the hard times and didn't need an extra burden. Edna had six children and many grand-children scattered throughout the country, but the depression made it almost impossible for any of them to care for her. And Edna had no desire to be taken care of. She had always worked, and although she knew she was slowing down, she was still strong enough for a full day's work.

She pushed herself off the seat, moved into the sunlight, and immediately began sweating. She sighed; the sun had been up only a couple of hours and it was already blazing hot. Iowa's summer weather was no better than Louisiana's, where she had spent her entire life until the death of her husband. She walked along the side of the road and squinted into the distance. She thought she could see the junction of the road that would take her to the farmhouse. It didn't look that far, and she quickened her pace.

After walking as briskly as she could, the road looked just as far off, and she slowed and panted to get her breath. She heard a motor behind her, and moved as close to the edge of the road as the weeds would allow. The motor became louder and a flatbed truck stopped a few yards in front of her. Her spirits rose, thinking that she would be offered a ride. Instead a man jumped off the truck bed, approached her, and said through a toothless mouth, "Think you're going to get away, nigger bitch?"

Edna's mouth dropped in shock, and she stammered that she wasn't "getting away." This annoyed the man, who slapped her full in the face. The slap stung and brought her to the realization that the man meant to harm her. Edna doubled her fist and caught the man on the side of his nose with a blow that had the force of all her strength and weight. Blood spurted, the man fell on his back and stayed there, and Edna felt a sharp pain in her fingers. Two other men had exited the cab of the truck, and they laughed uproariously at the plight of their companion.

"Jesus Christ, Clyde got knocked on his ass by a woman," chortled the driver. To the passenger he said, "Get his sorry ass into the truck and give him a shot of whiskey. I'll get the nigger loaded."

The passenger gathered up the toothless man, and the driver, not wishing a similar fate, slipped a revolver from the back of his pants and motioned Edna on to the truck bed. Knowing she was beaten, Edna slowly climbed in and sat with her back against the cab as she was directed. Her hand throbbed and her knuckles were bleeding, and she tucked it under her right arm and prayed silently as the truck roared off.

A black man with his hands tied to a hook over his head sat next to her. His mouth flicked a smile and he gave a small nod as the truck roared off. Edna wanted to ask him what was happening, but the man who squatted a few feet away from them with a rifle across his knees, discouraged any conversation.

Within a mile the truck stopped again and Edna watched as the toothless man, who had been revived by the whiskey and stinging from his ignominious defeat, approached a pregnant girl who was walking by the side of the road. He cursed the girl as a slut and knocked her to the ground. The girl

attempted to cover her head and stomach, but the man continued to pummel her until his companions pulled him off.
They roughly pushed her into the truck and sat her next to
Edna. The toothless man charged at both of them, but was
restrained by the driver, who said "All right, Clyde, you already proved you're a man." Clyde strutted to the cab cursing
Edna, and the truck roared off again.

The truck pulled off the main road onto one of rutted
dirt, and Edna and the girl jostled against each other. The girl
was whimpering against Edna's shoulder and holding her stomach, and Edna was afraid she would start labor. The truck
stopped and through the swirling dust Edna could see a two-
story house, a barn, and a tractor with a dozen or so men
standing by it. Some of the men were wearing sheets, and one
was holding a hood in his hand.

Edna understood: she was going to die.

5

John Peterson lay with his eyes closed in the spot where he had
been shoved and kicked. He knew that he was in a barn, and
the smell of the horses comforted him; he let his mind go to
the dusty plains of west Texas. When he opened his eyes, he saw
slivers of light through chinks in the barn's roof. From that
dim light he could see other people around him. Their hands
and feet were tied, just as his were. Next to him were the large
black woman and the pregnant girl. The girl's head was on the
woman's lap, and he could hear her soothing words as the girl
wimpered. Across from him was a black man about John's age,
a woman he thought might be Mexican, and a young white
woman. The black man caught John's eye and smiled.

"Got you all, too," he said. "Hard luck."

"What the hell is going on?" John asked. "What's going to happen to us?"

"They're the Klan, friend. That's what's going on. You know the Klan, don't you?"

John nodded. He'd spent most of his live with horses and his men, and he'd never seen a Klan member, but he'd read about them, seen pictures, and heard stories.

"Then I suspect you know we ain't being invited to dinner," the man said.

John nodded again. "My name's John. I'm from Texas."

"I'm Douglas. I suspect I'm from just about everywhere, but I was born in Alabama. This lady here"—he jerked his head to the right—"is called Floating Cloud. She's a real Sioux Indian, from South Dakota. Says that most people call her Sue. Sort of a play on her name. Best I can figure, this other lady's anme is Mary. She's kind of touched. She's got something wrong with her teeth; complains they hurt all the time. Thinks those men in the white robes are gonna fix 'em for her." Douglas raised his knees and leaned into them. "We were all at the camp by the tracks. Fire started and Klansmen were chagin people all over. We ran the wrong way—right into a hay wagon where a bunch of those sheeted devils were just waiting for us. Hard luck." He shook his head. "What be you ladies' names?"

"I'm Edna. I came down on the bus from Perry. I was hoping to get a job today. They got me off the road. Got this poor child, too. Like to have killed her."

"The girl turned her head and said, "My name is Betty. She whimpered and buried her head in Edna's lap.

"Edna busted one of them good," John said. "Bloodied his nose and knocked him clean on his back. Looked like a rag doll."

Douglas smiled. "Good for you, Edna. I hope I get just one chance to do the same."

Little other conversation passed amoung them as the barn warmed and the slivers of light grew brighter. All of them, except for Mary, knew their fates. John heard Douglas hum a spiritual, and Floating Cloud chanted something, under her breath. Edna alternately prayed and soothed Betty. John tried to pray, too, but he couldn't remember any prayers. He hoped that Edna's prayers would count for him, and he let his mind dream of Texas.

When two men opened the barn door to the mid-day sun, he knew his dreams were over.

6

Noah felt like whooping and jumping around his farmyard. The camp was burned, and they had captured six of the vermin. Vermin just for his pleasure. His loins tingled, and he could hardly contain himself, but he did. He mounted the truck bed and called the remaining men to his attention. He solemnly congratulated them on their victory, saying that their courageous actions had saved Bishop from the perverted decadence of these undesirables. By this deed the county of Bishop was safe for all decent Christian men, women, and children. He promised equally swift action against any other undesirables and bid the men return to their homes. Noah stepped off the bed and was greeted with handshakes and backslaps. He enjoyed the adulation, but was happier to see the last man ride down his lane and out of sight. He turned to Joe and said, "Now we can have some fun. Let's get something to eat and get my gear together."

Noah's gear, to Joe's surprise, consisted of his camera equipment. Joe knew that Noah took and developed pictures for a hobby with some attractive results, but he could fathom no use for such equipment in the present situation. Nonetheless, he carefully packed the camera, film, and flash into a wooden box. Unable to find its lid he used one of the several lattices that Noah's mother wove from apple tree prunings and set the box in the cab of the truck.

Noah added a couple of lanterns and the last whiskey jug and said, "Let's get our playmates."

Noah flung open the door to the barn and allowed his eyes to adjust to its dimness. As the figures sprawled on the floor became visible, he could no longer contain his excitement, and he let out a whoop. The whoop got everyone's attention, and they squinted against the sunlight to stare at him. He felt his power, and he grabbed a knife from the work bench and cut the ropes that bound their legs. He instructed Joe to help them up and load them on the truck, and he watched as they paraded past him. Their eyes, as they glanced at him, were frightened, and he felt his power and desire grow.

Joe started the truck, and guided it down Noah's rutted lane. When he reached the graveled road he asked, "Where we going?"

Noah took a sip from the jug. "We're going to that hotel on the lake that closed up last year. And we are going to make ourselves legends."

Joe didn't know how they could become legends, but he took a pull from the jug and headed the truck north.

7

Pain stabbed Joe's right eye, and he staggered backwards, trying to grab a hold on the rails of the side guards. He was unsuccessful, and he fell from the truck bed and thudded onto his back. The blow and fall dazed him, and he was momentarily confused as to why he was on his back.

By the time he scrambled to his feet his clarity returned. He knew that he and Noah had unloaded the two men and two of the women from the truck, and Noah had pushed them in the direction of the hotel, leaving him with the pregnant girl and the black woman. He had already gotten the girl off the truck and sent her after the others. The black woman must have worked her hands loose, and when he'd bent to get her up, she had hit him.

As soon as Joe had his thoughts straight, a bellow to the right of him demanded his attention. The two black men were charging him, and one was only a few yards from him. His head was lowered like a bull, and Joe could see the sweat glistening in his short, curly hair. Joe's first impulse was to run, but he countermanded that instinct and fumbled on his belt for the pistol Noah had given him. He grasped its handle, jerked it in front of him and fired. The man fell inches from Joe's feet. Joe was astonished that he had shot the man, and he stared at the blood staining the man's shirt. Joe's astonishment was short-lived because the second man hit him with his head and shoulders squarely in the chest. The blow knocked the gun from his hand and sent him sprawling. Before he could regain his feet, the man was on top of him, using his knees and shoulders to pummel him. Joe tried to squirm away, but the man outweighed him and was strong. Two sharp blows from the man's knee knocked his wind from him, and he lay helplessly gasping for air. He saw the man get to his feet and retract a foot to kick him. Still unable to move, Joe grimaced against the blow.

The blow didn't come, and when Joe opened his eyes he saw the man lying next to him and Noah standing over him with a rock in his hand.

Noah tossed the rock away and bent to retrieve the gun. He pointed it at Edna, who had climbed from the truck and was headed form them. The gun subdued her, and she joined the three other women to be herded toward the hotel. Noah called over his shoulder to Joe, "Get your breath and meet me inside."

Joe bent with his hands on his knees until he could breathe regularly. He brushed the dead weeds and grass from his clothes and looked for the gun. He picked it up and glanced at the man who had attacked him. He saw blood soaking into his hair and collar and knew that he was dead. *It was almost me,* he thought, and shuddered. He stuck the gun in his belt, smoothed his twisted shirt, and walked to the truck and sat on the running board. He shook grass from his hair and became aware of the sharp pain around his eye. *Bitch really hit me*, he thought, and touched the bruise gently. He could feel the swelling and the stabs of pain at his slightest touch. He took a long pull from the whiskey jug and felt it burn on its way to his stomach. He took a second one and walked unsteadily into the hotel. The door was open and a broken chain and crowbar rested on the tile floor inside the threshold. Joe walked through the door and up a short flight of stairs to an empty lobby. "Noah," Joe shouted, "you in here?"

Noah appeared at the top of the staircase to the second floor. "Got your air back? Come on up. Fun's still going on."

Joe wasn't sure he could take any more fun, but he leaned heavily on the rail and climbed the stairs. Noah led him into the first room, but Joe was unable to see anything. He thought he was blacking out until he realized that the room was windowless and that only the weak light from the lobby came through the door. When his eyes adjusted, he saw two women: Betty, the preganant girl, was on the bed; Edna, the black woman who had hit him, sat on the floor. As his eyes adjusted more he saw that the pregnant girl was naked except for a slip that was pushed under her breasts. The pale light shone on her heavy breasts. Their nipples were large, and although he couldn't see their color, Joe was certain that they were pink. He wanted to touch them.

Noah read his mind. "Go ahead. Who's going to stop you?" He laughed and grabbed the girl's right breast and squeezed it several times.

Joe, who had little sexual experience beyond the habits of chickens and cattle, thought Noah's behavior peculiar, but the naked breasts attracted him, and he reached out and stroked them lightly.

"That's it," Noah approved. "Get yourself a good feel. Stick your finger inside her, too."

Joe took the suggestion and was using all his fingers to explore her vagina when he heard, "You sick. Feeling a dead girl like that."

Joe jerked his hand away and turned to the source of the words: the black lady. Her eyes bulged and her lower lip quivered, but her voice was steady. "You both sick, and you both going to burn in hell."

Joe wondered what she was talking about; the girl wasn't dead. At least, she didn't feel dead.

He didn't have time to consider this further because Noah had slammed a pillow over the woman's face and pushed her to the floor. "Ain't no nigger bitch calling me sick. I'm going to have you when you're dead. Grab her arms, Joe."

Joe obediently seized the woman's flailing arms and watched Noah hold the pillow over her face with all of his weight. Her arms became limp and Joe smelled urine, and he knew that she was dead.

The thought that the girl might *really* be dead, too, slammed into his mind, and sickened him. He felt the whiskey burning the back of his throat, and he dry- swallowed to keep from vomiting. He couldn't stop it, and he dashed from the room. He got as far as the stair railing before spewing the alcohol-soaked contents of his stomach on the floor of the lobby. Joe was still gagging and spitting when he felt Noah's hand on his shoulder.

"Feel better?" he asked.

Joe wiped his mouth and nodded.

"Good. Get some air and get the box and lanterns from the truck."

Joe nodded again and forced a grin to show Noah that he was still with him. As he descended the stairs one at a time he wondered if he was sick for touching the dead girl. He told himself that he wasn't *really* sure she was dead, so it didn't matter. Besides, the thought of her naked breasts still excited him. He retrieved the box and the lanterns and finished the whiskey. He winched as it hit his now empty stomach, and by the time he reached the top of the stairs he was lightheaded and staggering.

He set the box inside the door and saw that the black woman was now naked except for a white undergarment below her large breasts. Her legs were spread, and he could see the pink inner flesh of her vagina. He remembered that Noah had said that he was going to screw her. He glanced at Noah's groin, which seemed large to him, and he supposed that Noah had already done it.

Noah went immediately to the box, tossed the makeshift lid aside, and began extracting his equipment. Joe staggered a few steps to the bed. With his vision blurred from the whiskey and his swollen eye, the girl certainly didn't *look* dead. He yielded to his desire to fondle her breasts again. She didn't feel dead either, and he felt his penis growing. He had never been with a woman, and he wanted this one.

"Go ahead. Take her," he heard Noah say from across the room. "I did and she was good."

Whiskey and lust broke the last of Joe's inhibitions, and he dropped his pants and mounted her. He thrust his penis into her, and after a few quick strokes, exploded. He rested his head on her breasts, panted, and swallowed to control his rolling stomach.

"Pull up your pants and help me with the nigger," Noah said behind him. He had pulled the black woman to a sitting position and had his arms hooked under her arms. "Grab her legs," he instructed. "I want her on the bed, too."

Joe buttoned his pants over his still erect penis, and he and Noah lifted the woman onto the bed. "Fix them so they face each other and put their hands on each other's tits," he said. Joe complied, and when he straightened he was surprised to see Noah had lit the lanterns and was adjusting his camera.

"What are you going to do?" he asked.

"Take some pictures that will save us and empower us. I'm going to show how perverted these vermin are. Then nobody will fault us for exterminating them, and other decent people will join us to stop them."

Joe, who was still drunk, vaguely realized that he had killed a man and helped kill a woman. A chill of fear shuddered through him until he understood that Noah's pictures would protect him. He didn't understand how, but he accepted it and unsteadily stepped out of the camera's view.

"Move them so their pussies touch," Noah said after a flash of light.

Joe arranged the bodies and stood back. The heat from the lanterns added to the already hot room, and Joe was sweating profusely.

"Stick the nigger's head on the other bitch's pussy," Noah said. "See if you can get her tongue out like she's licking it."

Joe was able to place the black woman's head, but although he pulled on it several times, he was unable to get her tongue to stay out of her mouth. He looked up helplessly at Noah.

"Just stick her face on it. It'll look good enough." After a flash of light he said, "Leave them. Let's get the bucks up here. I can do more with them." Noah lowered the lanterns and descended the stairs, and Joe staggered after him.

Joe clasped Douglas, the man he had shot, under his arms and around his chest, and began to drag him to the hotel. After a few steps, the pressure of Joe's arms caused Douglas' wound to spurt blood. Repelled and sickened, Joe dropped the man, gagged, and furiously wiped his hands on the grass. He grabbed Douglas' ankles and pulled him llike a rickshaw across the grass and up the stairs.

Noah had lugged John in the same fashion, to avoid the blood that leaked from the back of John's head. Both Noah and Joe panted and heaved from the exertion. Joe had sweat-out most of the whiskey and he felt somewhat sober.

"You put yours in that room over there," Noah said, after he caught his breath. "Mine's going in here." Noah nodded to an open door a few feet away. "Come back so you can help me."

Joe grunted and pulled Douglas to the room Noah had indicated. It was like the other room: small, windowless, and dark. He made out the figure of Floating Cloud on the bed; she was naked except for a sock that dangled off her right foot. Joe tentatively brushed his finger against her side. She felt cool, and he knew that she was dead. Joe didn't like to touch dead things, least of all humans, and he rubbed his finger on his pants to cleanse it. Noah mush have killed her with the pillow, like the black woman. That meant that the other girl was dead, too.

Joe leaned against the wall and thought his first sober thoughts in several hours. The killing of the two men didn't bother him; after all, they had attacked him. But none of the women had except the black woman, and she had only hit him in his eye. He didn't understand why they needed to die, especially the girl that was pregnant. Thinking of the girl caused him to remember something horribly repulsive to him. Was it possible he had had sex with a dead girl? He recalled touching her breasts, and he saw that a couple of buttons on his pants were undone, but he couldn't believe that his first sexual encounter had been with a dead girl. He dry-wretched and put the thought from his mind. He did recall moving the naked women around the bed and that memory disgusted him. He rubbed his hands vigorously on his pants to clean them.

Noah was busy moving his camera equipment into the room and called to Joe to bring the lanterns. When Joe returned with them, Noah had already stripped the man, and was using a scrap of underwear to wipe the blood off the torso.

"Don't think this blood will show much because this is one black nigger, but I don't want to spoil the picture. Help me hoist him onto the bed," Noah demanded.

Joe gingerly gripped the man's ankles, lifted, and again rubbed his hands on his pants. He deliberately stood as far from the bed as possible and hoped that Noah would position the bodies without his help. Noah took a couple of pictures with the man on top of the woman and said, "Let's turn her over like a dog."

Joe complied, but touched as little of the dead flesh as possible. Noah was able to position the woman on her hands and knees with her vagina exposed from the rear, but was unable to keep the man in a kneeling position behind her. No matter how he tried to balance him, he slumped to one side or the other.

"Just need a little something to keep him up," Noah muttered to himself and looked around the room. His eyes lit on the carpet that was unraveled by the door. He yanked it off the floor, ripped it, and pulled a long cord from the frayed end. "We can tie him upright. Loop an end of this around the light socket in the ceiling, and I'll put the other end around his neck."

Relieved that he didn't have to touch the man, Joe stood on the small dresser and tied the cord to the light socket, and Noah grabbed the opposite end and secured it around the man's neck. To Joe's surprise, the cord held him upright, and Noah pushed the man's groin into the woman's buttocks. He shook his head. "Doesn't look real. Wish he could really get his cock into her. Maybe I can shove it in." He set down his camera and tried to direct the man's penis into the woman. "Needs to be hard," he said and began to pump the man's penis. "Maybe this will get it."

Joe, at this point, had seen all he could stand. He was sober now, and he knew that what Noah was doing was unnatural. He didn't think that it was natural for Noah to have a huge bulge in his pants, either. He backed to the door, saw Noah trying to stick the limp penis into the woman, saw the glint of pleasure in Noah's eyes, felt his stomach roll, and bolted down the stairs and outside.

He held onto the fender of the truck as he wretched dry heaves. His head throbbed both from the whiskey and his battered eye, and his throat and mouth burned from his stomach acid. He was exhausted from the last thirty physical and emotional hours, and he climbed onto the truck bed, lay in the patch of shade made by the cab, and passed out.

When he awoke, the truck was moving, and through his good eye he recognized the gravel road that passed by his farm and Noah's. The shadows of the trees stretched across the road, which told him it was early evening. A pile of clothes was beside him, and he assumed that they must be from the people they had killed. He moved away from them. Within minutes Noah turned into his lane and stopped the truck. Joe climbed off the bed and steadied himself.

Noah was already out of the cab; his eyes were gleaming and he said, "Boy, we really did it. We showed those vermin who's in charge." He grabbed his camera from the seat. "When I get these pictures developed there won't be any doubt about it, and we and the rest of the Klan will be royalty in Bishop. We'll be too powerful for anyone to cross." He laughed. "You should have been with me with that last pair. Got my best pictures there. That buck was hung like a horse, and I swear that anyone would think that he was inside her. Lit my fire, and I had her, too. That white bitch was the best one of all. Nice and slim. SMooth, cool skin." He gave Joe a nudge in his side.

Joe didn't understand how any of what they'd done would make them powerful, and he forced all thoughts of it from his mind. He heard Noah ask him to burn the clothes; he gathered them from the truck bed, and Noah drove off. Joe looked dumbly at the clothes, feeling his legs shake. The thought "burn them" bounced in his mind, and he walked behind his barn and soaked them with kerosene. He had struck a match when the boots caught his eye. They were nice boots, far too good to burn, except the heels looked loose. He knew he could easily fix those and pulled them from the pile. He struck another match, set the pile on fire, and went into the barn to examine the boots. The heels just needed a couple of nails to be good as new, but he saw the edge of something wedged against the sole. He used a screwdriver to pull it out and found it was a ten dollar bill. Excited, he grabbed the other boot, wrenched the heel off, and pulled out a second bill. Twenty dollars; he was rich. He stuffed them into his pocket, and feeling much better, walked to his bed and collapsed into sleep.

8

When Joe woke the next morning his eye was swollen shut and his head hurt, and he was hungry. In the kitchen he used the sink pump to wash, and looked for something to eat. He saw a plate of biscuits that his mother had left on the table. He spread bacon grease on two of them and wolfed them down. They filled his stomach, and he felt better. He smoothed his clothes and felt the two ten dollar bills in his pocket. He took them out and spread them on the table and stared at them. It was a small fortune, some good food, a dress for his mother, and pair of shoes, and plenty left over for fun. He spread some grease on a third biscuit and slowly ate it. Thinking about fun reminded him of the fun that Noah had provided for him, and the biscuits turned sour in his stomach. He stared at the bills some more, then stuck one under the plate for his mother to find and shoved the other one into his pocket. He went outside, poured some gas into the car his father had purchased ten years ago, cranked it to life, and drove to town.

Joe used most of his money at the hardware store to buy

plaster mix, lath, paint, and a brush and trowel. He used a dollar more at the gas station to purchase three gallons of gas and a quart of oil for the car and two bottles of Coca-Cola for himself. He drove out of Bishop and along the lake until he came to the road that led to the hotel. He slowed and guided the car through the ruts and weeds of the neglected road. When the hotel came into view he stopped and finished the last of his first Coke, placing the bottle on the seat to claim the deposit later.

When the hotel had been built, Joe had been in his late teens and a farmer who had never left Bishop County. The hotel had represented luxury and sophistication to him, and Joe had wanted more than anything to stay there and be a part of that life. Now, five years later, he didn't know if he could force himself to go in it again.

The lobby smelled of death and vomit as Joe lugged his supplies to the second floor. He was grateful that the doors to all three rooms were closed, and he kept them closed as he removed their moldings and nailed lath over their faces. Joe had learned to plaster when he had helped Bishop's contractor build several houses three years ago. Times had been good then, but now the contractor was out of business and the houses were empty. He applied the plaster in two layers over the lath and smoothed the last layer flush to the wall. He replaced his supplies in the car and opened his second Coke. He'd return in a couple of days to sand and paint the plaster. Joe was good at this type of work, and he believed that when he was finished no one would be able to tell that the doorways had ever existed. That was the way he wanted the last two days of his life to be—like they had never existed.

9

Two days after Joe painted the sealed doorways Noah called a Klan meeting, and both men again stood on the truck bed surrounded by torches. Noah was preaching and pounding his Bible to emphasize his points; Joe was not listening. Instead, he was trying to count the size of the audience. This was not an easy task since it was dark and men kept arriving and moving around. He had tried three times and had reached sixty on the last try, but guessed there could be thirty more. Nearly a hundred men had come to hear Noah. Joe was amazed; only the county fair brought out such a crowd.

When Noah finished preaching he handed Joe some papers and told him to pass them around. He announced to the crowd that they were going to see the kind of degenerates they had to save Bishop from. He warned them that the pictures showed unspeakable sexual acts and said they didn't have to look. The men fairly grabbed the pictures from Joe and moved into the torch light to look at them. Joe didn't need to look; he had already seen the real thing, and it didn't exist for him anymore.

Noah's power grew with the Klan through the rest of the summer, and by fall its membership included the mayor, sheriff, county councilmen, and most businessmen. But its power couldn't control nature or the economy, and with a poor harvest, Joe and his mother lost their farm in late October. The sale of their car provided money for a train ticket to Chicago for his mother where she had arranged to live with her sister. Joe was left with his clothes and a few dollars and became part of that transient group scattered over the rails and highways that he had helped to destroy, kill, and defile. Fortunately for Joe, he was able to seal those memories in a corner of his mind as neatly as he had sealed seven lives in an old hotel.

CHAPTER THIRTEEN

The dance marked the unofficial end of summer. The weekend was cool and rainy, and most of the tourists departed to prepare for the start of school. The ER on Monday was lighter than usual, and I spent most of the day in my office doing paper work. I had cleared my desk of everything but my ninety-eight photos of the skeletons, which wouldn't fit into my file. I decided to sort out the extraneous ones of the rooms and hallways and file only the ones of the skeletons themselves. For lack of anything better to do with the extra pictures, I took them home.

Paul was packing a satchel when I arrived home. "Want to get an early start in the morning," he said.

"Oh, yeah. You're going to Cedar Falls. Need anything?"

"Don't think so. Probably be back late Wednesday."

"Okay. You eat?"

He nodded. "At the lodge. Mrs. Harden asked about you today."

"Yeah? What'd she say?" I feigned disinterest, but my voice betrayed me.

"Oh, just stuff." Paul's eyes were dancing.

"What kind of stuff?" I demanded.

"She asked what kind of doctor you were, where you got your car, and if you were seeing anyone special."

"No kidding." I was almost gleeful. "What did you tell her?"

"That you work in the emergency room, bought your car in California ..."

"Not that. About seeing anyone."

"Well, I had to say no."

"Good. But what'd she say then?" This was maddening.

"To call her. She told me to remind you to call her. She said she's in her office until five. I told you she meant it."

"I'll be damned." I remembered her head on my shoulder.

"So you going to call her?" asked Paul.

"Yeah. Tomorrow."

"Promise?"

"Yeah, I promise." I looked at Paul's dancing eyes. "Give me a break. Damned matchmaker." I heard him chuckling as I went into the kitchen and made some soup.

"What are these pictures?" Paul picked the bundle off the coffee table.

I swallowed some soup. "They're the ones I took of the rooms where the skeletons were. Didn't have room in my file for those. Take a look if you want."

Paul spread some pictures on the table. "They were really walled in, weren't they? Never would have known they were there without tearing the place down."

"That's about it," I said and spooned the last of the soup into my mouth.

"What's this?" Paul asked.

I squinted at the picture. "That's the light in the ceiling. I took pictures of the whole room."

"No, I mean this." Paul pointed to a place on the picture that I couldn't see. I got up and examined it under the table lamp.

"Looks like a string. Probably the pull cord for the light."

"I don't think so. See, here's the chain for the cord on this side of the bulb. This string's on the other side."

"Yeah, you're right," I said. "I wonder why that was there."

"Maybe somebody was hanged," Paul suggested.

"I don't think the light or the string would be strong enough. Besides, the skeleton right below this light belongs to a man who had been shot."

"Maybe it held him up somehow after he was dead," Paul ventured.

"Could have done that, I guess. But he was found lying on top of the other skeleton." I remembered the folded legs and the vertebrae sticking up from the bed. "He didn't start out like that. I'll bet he was kneeling and that string kept him upright. The string rotted away, and he fell forward. But why would anyone do that?"

"I don't know," said Paul. "But whoever did this weren't ordinary people. Maybe they wanted to look at their handy work awhile before they sealed the room."

The image of men, or women, or both standing around looking at two dead bodies in a tiny hotel room was unsettlingly morbid.

"Suppose they took pictures, too," I said, half to myself.

"I guess they could have," Paul said.

"Could have what?" I asked.

"What you just said. Taken pictures."

"I really didn't mean ..." I stopped. If that string held the dead male upright, he was posed. If someone was going to pose a dead body, it was going to be recorded. "I'll bet to hell and gone they did take pictures." For the first time I realized that the positions of the bones on the beds were not the results of randomly falling dead bodies, but arrangements of macabre portraits. "I think I'm going to go to my office and get a closer look at the pictures of the skeletons."

"I think I'll go with you," Paul said.

***

"Okay, let's see what we got here," I said, as Paul and I huddled over the pictures of the skeletons spread on my desk. "The two in the first room would have been," I checked my notes, "an Indian woman face down on the bed with a black man kneeling behind her. Strange pose."

"Yeah," Paul agreed.

I consulted my notes again. "In the second room a white woman was lying face up with a black man face down on top. Guess he could have been kneeling originally. The third room had the pregnant girl. She was on her back, and the large black woman was kneeling over the bed, and, I guess, over the pregnant girl. Black woman's head ended up between the girl's legs. All pretty unusual."

"Yeah. Could the black woman's head have been shoved between the legs on purpose?" Paul asked.

"No reason why not, but that would have been stranger yet. Like they were having sex."

"Maybe these are sex poses," said Paul. "Did you find any clothes?"

"Some fibers on the bones and some buttons was all. They

could have been nearly nude. Shit, maybe you've got something. The first pair could have been posed doggie style; the second pair could have been in the missionary position, and the last pair looks like lesbian oral sex. Jesus."

"Interracial sex would have been pretty controversial sixty years ago," said Paul.

"Still controversial now for many people. Would have been a taboo then. In fact, lesbian sex and doggie style are still taboo for some people. These would have been some real shockers. And these were just the final poses."

"What do you mean?"

"Takes about four hours for a body to start to get stiff. Nearly twelve hours for it to be completely rigid. Whoever killed them could have devised lots of poses in that amount of time."

"Shit, they had to be total kinks," said Paul.

"You're right there. I'm going to show these to Bird tomorrow. You're a pretty good detective. Maybe you should try a criminology major instead of business." I gave Paul a shot in the arm, and he grinned.

Bird was unenthused by Paul's discovery. "So somebody took some freaky pictures. Still doesn't give us a single clue about who killed them."

"Bird, if someone took the pictures, someone had to develop them, and someone looked at them."

"Fine. Think I can go down to the drug store and ask to see their photography customers for the last sixty years? Drug store wasn't even there sixty years ago."

"Well, who developed the pictures then?"

Bird stretched his arms. "I don't have any idea and no way to find out. For godsakes, Bill, sixty years is a long time. If you want to try, go ahead, it's an open case. Now, you want to get some lunch or what?"

***

After lunch I retreated to my office and dialed Emily's number. At least, I figured, if I bombed, I would do it in private. Her secretary answered and put me on hold.

"Emily Harden." Her voice had a business tone, and I forgot my well-rehearsed lines.

"Uh, this is Bill, Emily. I gave you a ride from the dance. You said I should call you."

I heard the rustling of paper and background conversation. "Bill," she said with recognition. "I'm glad you called. Could you pick me up at the lodge at five-thirty today? My car is finished, and I need a ride to the garage."

"Yeah, sure."

"You're a dear. See you then."

I hung up the phone. This was not the conversation that I had expected, and I knew I had gotten my hopes up for nothing. She only needed a ride. She wanted me to call so I could give her a ride. Her head on my chest and shoulder had been the actions of an exhausted woman who probably didn't even remember them. I kicked the door jam and limped back to the ER, confused by women and more confused about why I cared enough to kick a door jam.

Emily emerged from the lodge entrance and scanned the parking lot. I saw her speak to the parking attendant. He shook his head, and she disappeared into the lodge. I realized that she was looking for the Mercury, not a county van, and I followed her into the lodge.

"Emily," I called to her as she was inserting a key into her office door.

"There you are. I was going to call you." She placed her hand on my arm and patted it. I wasn't sure if this was affection, but I liked it and dutifully guided her to the van.

"Where's your car?" she asked when I opened the door of the van. "I wanted to see it again."

"Home. This is my county van. I use it for work."

She looked at "Medical Examiner" stenciled on the side and asked, "Do you carry dead bodies in this?"

"Not lately," I said and closed the door.

"Your car at Johnny's?" I asked, as I pulled out of the drive.

"That's right. I really appreciate this ride again. You must think I'm an awful nuisance."

If she just wanted the ride the answer was "yes," I thought, but said, "Not at all."

She stretched her legs and loosened her high heels. I looked. "If you don't have plans maybe I could pay you back with dinner."

"You don't need to do that," I said and thought: *what an idiot.* "I don't have plans, though," I added quickly.

"Good," she said. "I started a stew in the crock pot this morning. It should be done. Stew's all right, isn't it?"

"Stew's fine," I said.

"Then follow me out to my house as soon as I pick up my car."

I wasn't exactly riding on air as I followed Emily, but I felt pretty good, and I hoped that the dinner invitation was because she wanted my company, not a pay back for the rides. I parked next to her in front of the garage. Pansy cocked her head and studied me, then smelled my hand and nuzzled my leg.

"That dog was supposed to protect me," Emily said. "Well, come in."

Emily, I could readily see, was a clean freak. The kitchen floor shone, as did the counter tops. The sink was pearly white and devoid of dishes. The living room carpet was spotless, the couch had symmetrically placed pillows, and the tables and bookshelves would pass a white glove test.

"My God. I'm afraid to sit down. My house doesn't look anything like this," I said.

"Don't be silly. Sit where you want. I just cleaned this morning; it's usually pretty messy. I'm going to get into some comfortable shoes." She disappeared down the hall, and I heard a door close.

I sat on the couch, trying not to disturb the pillows. I was certain that when Emily's house was messy, it would be in better condition than mine, which was littered with books, magazines, dishes, and clothes. I was trying to remember when I last mopped my kitchen floor when Emily reappeared.

"You changed more than your shoes," I said. I had no idea what Emily was wearing was called, but it was red, soft, and shiny. The top part was edged with a rose-patterned lace that revealed an inch or so of cleavage. The bottom extended in loose folds to her slippers, but was slit on both sides to show her calves. She had unpinned her hair, and it flowed in gray-streaked chestnut waves to her shoulders.

"Do you like this?" she asked. "It's really comfortable after being in a suit and heels all day."

"You look great."

She patted my arm. "You're sweet. I'm going to warm some bread and then we can eat. You can freshen up in the bathroom down the hall."

I watched her walk into the kitchen, and I wasn't thinking about food. I splashed handfuls of cold water on my face in the bathroom. I had not been attracted to a woman since my divorce and had accommodated my sexual urges with one night stands, prostitutes, or alone. I was unaccustomed to this feeling, and was unsteady and disoriented. "Try not to be completely stupid," I said to my reflection.

The aroma of Emily's stew and bread restored my appetite. Her table afforded a view of the road and the fields beyond, and she had set it with crystal goblets, china, and candles.

"I know stew and candles don't mix, but I like a nice table, and I feel silly doing it for myself."

"Don't apologize. It's nice. Romantic."

She smiled.

Romantic or not, I managed to consume three plates of stew and half a loaf of bread.

"Lord," she said as she cleared the table. "You eat like my son. You'd think you'd never had stew before."

"Not like that," I said. "It's a whole lot better than the stuff in the can."

She stopped with the plates in her hands. "That's what you eat? Canned food?"

"Well, yeah. That and sandwiches and in restaurants. I do make a good breakfast, though," I said, feeling a little defensive.

She shook her head, and I watched the chestnut waves tumble. "It's a wonder you have any meat on you at all."

"Does your son live with you?" I asked, eager to change the subject.

"Oh, no. He lives in New York. When he graduated from college he went to work for an investment company. Two years later he was transferred to New York. His picture is on the book shelf."

I walked to the shelf and squinted at the picture. The

image of an older man was next to it. "Is the other picture of your husband?"

Emily joined me by the shelf. She touched the top of the frame. "He died of cancer five years ago. We ran this farm together until then." Her head wagged a little. "Then I rented the fields and started working at the lodge. I kept the house, though. Too many memories to give up." She touched the frame again. "Sometimes I'm over it, and sometimes I'm not. You know what I mean?"

I nodded.

"Well," Emily tossed a towel to me. "You want to dry the dishes?"

Whatever efforts I performed in drying were purely mechanical. I was completely engrossed in the light reflecting off strands of Emily's hair, her perfume, and her body sliding under its shiny red covering. After the dishes had been returned to their stacks in the cabinets, she fixed brandy for me and tea for herself. We sipped our drinks at the table and watched the landscape fade into the shadows of night. Emily's proximity was unnerving, and the brandy failed to relax me.

"You always this tense?" she asked.

"No. I mean I'm sorry, I didn't know it showed. I got something on my mind."

"Help to talk about it?"

I set my drink on the table. Ignominious failure was better than my present torment. "Yeah, it would, but I'm not very good at this, and you're what's on my mind, Emily. I like you a lot, and I'm really attracted to you. Probably because you're pretty, but it's more than that, and I want to see you more and have a relationship with you. And I'm not just saying this as a line to get sex. That's not what I'm after. Well, it is but ... Christ Almighty, I don't know how to do this. I haven't had feelings like this in twenty years." I had been examining the table top during my soliloquy, and I dared a peek at Emily's face. To my relief, she was smiling. I hoped that she wouldn't start laughing.

"Bill, that's the nicest compliment I've heard in years. The most disorganized, but nicest." She patted my hand. "I'd like to get to know you better, too, and yes, I find you attractive."

For a few moments the world consisted only of Emily, me, and the dining room table. I crossed the table and held her in my arms. I moved my hands over the red satin and felt her body quiver underneath. My own muscles tensed at her touches and my senses were oblivious to any stimulation but hers. After a long probing kiss, she pushed back slightly.

"My God. I only met you four days ago. I don't get swept away like this."

"I know," I said. I pulled her close; she didn't resist.

"We just shouldn't do this on our first date."

"I know," I said and held her tighter.

She moved against my chest. "This could be our second date, though. You did bring me home Friday."

"I haven't had a second date in years and years."

She stroked my back. "They're the best ones."

When I drove home hours later, the stars were decidedly brighter.

CHAPTER FOURTEEN

In the morning, I made two calls. The first was to the hospital flower shop to have flowers delivered to Emily. I had no idea of the proper etiquette for the morning after, but I figured flowers couldn't hurt. I made the second call to Doctor Learner; Bird and the mayor may have lost interest in the skeletons, but I hadn't. My fictional scenarios no longer placated me; I wanted to know the truth about their lives and deaths, at least as much as I could. Besides, no one deserved the cold anonymity of the morgue as a final resting place.

Doctor Learner identified himself with the same soft voice, we exchanged greetings, and he inquired about his report.

"Your report was fine, Doctor, but it didn't help much with the identity of the skeletons."

"Given their age that might be too much to hope for," he said.

"Probably, but I read an article once about a technique that applies flesh-like substances to skulls to give an indication of the appearance of its owner. I think it was used to identify some of the victims of the guy from Chicago that buried young boys under his house. I wondered if you knew anything about that."

"I don't perform that technique myself, but I believe a young lady in Oklahoma is the reputed expert. If you'll hold, I'll try to locate her name and number."

Learner came back on with the name of Patricia Leighton. He gave me a phone number and apologized for not having the address and asked to be informed of the results. Doctor Learner, I thought as I hung up the phone, hadn't lost interest, either.

I left a message on Patricia Leighton's machine and provided her with my hospital and home numbers, and immediately became impatient for her return call. On my lunch break I decided to learn more about who developed pictures in the 'thirties, and I visited Ervin Johnston, figuring that newspapers had pictures and maybe Ervin knew something about past developers.

The *Bishop Reporter*, Ervin's paper, was housed in the old bank building. Although Ervin was the sole reporter, editor, and printer of the paper, the center portion of the building, where customers once lined up for tellers, was filled with several battered desks all used at various times by Ervin. The teller area itself, which still contained the cages, was occupied by printing presses, teletypes, and bundles of papers. Ervin was eating a banana at one of the rear desks when I entered. He raised a finger, indicating that I should wait. He finished his banana and moved to the desk at the front on which I saw a small sign reading CITY EDITOR. Ervin adjusted the chair and picked up a pencil.

"How may I help you?" he asked.

"I need a little information, Ervin. This paper in business in nineteen thirty?"

"My grandfather established the *Reporter* in nineteen nineteen after he returned from World War One. It was moved to its present facilities in nineteen thirty-three after the bank failed. It is a weekly paper under the complete ownership of the Johnston family."

"That's swell, Ervin," I said, suspecting that this could be a long process. "But what I'd like to know is who developed pictures for the paper around nineteen thirty."

Ervin put down his pencil, realizing that I didn't have a news story. "Nobody. We didn't print pictures until after World War Two. Those came in on the teletype."

"Oh. Well, do you know anyone in town that developed pictures then?"

"That was before my time, but I doubt that anyone did. Home photography wasn't that popular then, and the developing process was more complicated than now. I suspect whatever pictures people took were developed in Des Moines or Sioux City."

"Yeah. What about a portrait studio? Bishop have anything like that?"

"Not to my knowledge. People that wanted such a thing went to Des Moines or Sioux City."

That appeared to be a dead end, and I tried something else. "Do you have records of your papers from around nineteen thirty?"

"Got a record of every edition of the *Reporter* ever printed."

"Could I see them?"

"Sure. They're upstairs." Ervin led the way to a rear stair case; he donned a white, cloth hat, and we mounted the stairs. The second floor consisted of labyrinthine shelves piled with newspapers. The *Reporter* was not yet in the microfilm or the computer age.

"Careful of the rat traps," he warned, as we snaked through

the maze. "Rats just love newspapers. Okay, here's the 'thirties." He pointed to a mass of yellowed papers. "The 'forties start at this red mark here." He patted a swab of red paint on a shelf. "You looking for a particular one?"

I shook my head. "I'm not sure what I'm looking for." I checked my watch. "I've got to get back to work. Can I look through some of these later?"

"Public record. I'm here until five most of the time. This have something to do with those skeletons? Did you figure out who they were?"

"No. I was hoping some of those old papers would give me some clues."

We descended the stairs and Ervin exchanged his cloth hat for a green eye shade and snapped on the lights in his printing area. "Did you know," he asked as I was opening the door, "that devil worship was common in the 'thirties?"

"No, I didn't, Ervin."

"I think the hotel was built by devil worshipers and those skeletons were their sacrifices."

"Maybe, Ervin. See you later."

***

Emily called me in the ER and thanked me for the flowers and invited me to dinner that evening. I accepted, and we chatted a couple of minutes. When I hung up, Rosalee, the admitting nurse, looked at me with an open mouth.

"You made a date? The world must be ending."

"Second one this week," I said and winked at her.

I spent an hour after work in Ervin's second floor, scanning yellow, rat-chewed papers, and learned only that Ervin's grandfather had a penchant for stories about flying saucers, ghosts, and scandalous Democrats. Ervin came by his style rightly. I showered the mustiness off me, left a message for Paul, and drove to Emily's, where I ate four pieces of fried chicken.

"You're going to make me fat," I said and rubbed my full stomach.

"A few pounds won't hurt you," she said. "But don't get the idea that I'm going to feed you every night. I expect to be taken out sometimes." She tossed a curl out of her face. She was dressed in a black outfit similar to the red one, but with a slit in the front. It made her hair darker and contrasted wickedly with her red nails and lips. Lust was my dominant feeling.

"Sure," I said, although I preferred her flowing hair and the shiny material that softly encased her body to the business suits she wore in public. "We could go to Verne's on Friday."

"In you car," she added. "I want to ride in it when I'm awake."

"Okay. Listen, on Labor Day weekend Jackson County is having a fair in Perry, the county seat. Usual exhibits and carnival, but they're also having a car show on Saturday. I was going to take the Mercury, and I thought maybe you'd like to go. There should be some nice cars, and you can check out the rest of the fair if you get bored."

"I'd love to go, and I don't think I'll get bored." She patted my hand with her red nails. Lust took control, and I pulled her to me.

***

I didn't see Paul until the next morning. He told me that he and Cindy had found an apartment and that he had found a job in a hardware store. They planned to move this weekend, since his job started on Monday. Cindy's parents were giving them some furniture, and Cap Schmidt had volunteered the use of his truck. Paul asked for my help, and I assented.

"Hey," he asked as I started for the door, "did you call Mrs. Harden?"

I smiled. "Yes."

I realized as I saw the sun crack the horizon on my way to work that I had agreed to several hours of confinement in the cab of a truck with Cap Schmidt.

Emily called me before noon to inform me that I was on my own this evening because she had to interview for Paul's replacement, but she was looking forward to Friday's date.

"Another one?" asked Rosalee.

"Number three," I said.

She shook her head. "You're going to need vitamins, Doc."

I spent two lunch breaks with yellow newspapers before I found something. A short article on the second page stated that the sheriff's office was investigating the disappearance of a Jackson County woman. The woman's relatives stated that she had recently arrived in Perry from Louisiana and had gone to Bishop seeking work. The paper was dated October twelve, nineteen thirty-one, but the article failed to mention any names. I scanned several more issues but found nothing else that referred to it. I used one of Ervin's phones that rested on a desk labeled SPORTS to call Bird.

"Records from nineteen thirty-one? Shit, no. They'd have been pitched out long ago. We only go back twenty years or so. You still messing with those skeletons?"

"Thought maybe I could find something about who took the pictures."

"Hard head. You don't even know if anyone took pictures. Too much time passed. There's nothing to find anymore."

I was beginning to think that Bird was right. I had no idea where to look next, and Patricia Leighton hadn't called back.

***

My date with Emily on Friday was the perfect buffer for Cap on Saturday. Cap was a man of opinions and theories which he felt obligated to share. Except for the time when we passed a cattle feed yard, which caused him to slam his fist on the dash hard enough to open the glove compartment and curse corporate farming, I stayed insulated in chestnut curls, red nails, and the soft folds of Emily's body.

One of Cap's theories was that anyone who didn't farm was a weakling, and he was surprised that I didn't tire first when we unloaded the furniture. He called for a break and sat wheezing on the couch. I joined Paul outside.

"Pretty nice place," I said. "Can you afford it?"

"I think so. Once I finish my training at the store, I get a raise and a commission."

"I'm going to miss you. I liked having you around this summer. Be hard to be alone again."

"Yeah, I liked it, too, Dad. But Cedar Falls isn't that far away. We'll see each other."

"Been pretty proud of you, too. Working, taking responsibilities, and all that." I kicked the truck tire with my toe. "You grew up to be a good guy."

"Did most of it this summer," Paul grinned.

Leaving his daughter subdued Cap, and we rode home in silence.

***

The following week Emily and I shared dinners and ourselves when we could, and I readied the Mercury for the show. But the skeletons stayed in the back of my mind.

Perry is over sixty miles from Bishop, and I picked Emily up at dawn.

"I like to ride in your car when I'm awake," she yawned. "I don't know if I'll make it today. Do car shows always start this early?"

"Oh, yeah. In fact, we're getting kind of a late start."

"Why so early?" she asked and adjusted her head on my shoulder.

"Because," I said, "because ... I don't have any idea. They just do."

She snickered and began to breathe regularly.

Emily woke up when I paid my registration fee and helped me clean the car and set up the chairs and umbrella.

"I thought you polished this all week long," she said as she watched me shine the airplane hood ornament.

"I did, but it got dirty driving up here. I'm just touching up."

"And you call me a clean freak."

Emily and I spent the morning looking at the other cars, talking to my acquaintances, and wandering through the carnival. She talked me into a ride on the Ferris wheel during which I intently gripped the safety bar as she pointed out the sights below. We bought sandwiches and ate them by the car.

"This is fun. I've lived in Jackson County for years, and I've never been to their fair."

"Your place is in Jackson County?" I asked.

"The house is just over the line. But we were so much closer to Bishop we always went there for church and shopping and things."

To my surprise, I won a third place trophy in the 'fifties class when the awards were announced.

"Should have been first place," said Emily as we drove home.

"No. I was lucky to get third. That was a pretty small show, and I didn't have much competition. I've got quite a bit to do to the old car before it'll be first place quality. I didn't get much done on it this summer because I was fixing up Paul's car." I paused. "You know, he only lived with me a couple of months, but I really miss him."

"I know," said Emily. "I miss my son, too. But it does get better. Actually, I miss Paul, too. He was a reliable worker and good with the customers. You've got a nice son."

"Yes, I do," I said. "And I can say that objectively since I had precious little to do with raising him."

Emily rested against my shoulder. "Probably more than you think, Bill. A lot more."

CHAPTER FIFTEEN

I found a message on my machine from Patricia Leighton when I got home from work on Tuesday. She stated that she had just returned from a vacation and would be home all evening. I called and explained what I wanted.

"How many skulls are there?" she asked.

"Six and a fetus."

"I couldn't possibly do anything with a fetus except make it look like a doll, which would be of no use to you. I'm surprised that you have those type of remains."

"It was nearly full term and in a protected setting," I said.

"Still couldn't do anything worthwhile with it. Do you know the sex, race, or age of the others?"

"Yes, all that."

"I can sculpt a face to fit the skull, but I should warn you, it might not resemble the person's actual face very closely. There are many variables involved."

"I see. How do you do it, anyway?" I asked.

"It's like making a mask. First, I make a cast of the skulls, then I use clay and putty to build a face. There are several places on the human face where the flesh is at a specific depth. For example, the upper lip is about eleven millimeters thick, but the upper nose and forehead are only four millimeters thick. Applying the clay in the proper thicknesses on the cast will eventually result in a face. But, like I said, there are variables that more or less have to be guessed at, like mouth size, wrinkles, or sagging jowls and eyelids. I can make educated guesses knowing the person's age, race, and sex, but they're still guesses."

"Okay, but right now you're all I've got," I said. "How long would it take?"

"If I do it, and that is if, figure on at least a month each, given my present schedule. And I charge."

"How much?"

"Twenty-five hundred each."

"Oh." I knew that neither the mayor nor the county board would authorize that type of expenditure on a case that was only technically open. "I'm sorry I bothered you, Ms. Leighton. I couldn't get that kind of money. It was kind of a long shot, anyway."

"There is another possibility. I'm teaching a class in this technique at the University of Oklahoma this fall, and I will need skulls for my students to practice on. Do yours represent more than one race?"

"Yeah. There're two black men, and four women: two white, one black, and one Indian."

"That's quite a variety. I could accept your skulls as donations. I'll make casts for the students and return the skulls to you. But you must understand that the work will be done by students, and there won't be any results until the end of the class in October."

"That's great. How do I get them to you?"

"Individually boxed in Styrofoam is best. I recommend overnight delivery. Less jostling around. Send me anything you have like hair samples and descriptive information."

I took down her address. "I'll send them tomorrow afternoon. I really appreciate this, Ms. Leighton."

"Don't thank me yet. I don't know how they'll come out."

***

September brought an early fall. Leaves turned, the nightly choruses of insects disappeared, and gas stations advertised specials on winterizing cars. Lead stories and headlines pondered the fate of the corn crop in the cool weather.

I visited Paul once in Cedar Falls sans the accompaniment of Cap Schmidt's theories. He had finished his training period at the hardware store and was providing adequately for himself and Cindy. They seemed successful at cohabitation, and I figured that marriage would be next. I spent a few more lunch breaks reading Ervin's papers, but found only one article concerning the hotel, and that was in 1933 when the county board voted to lease part of it to the Moose Lodge. Seven others already had a life-time lease, I thought.

The last of the tourists departed, and the drone of ski boats were replaced by the sputtering motors of local anglers and the honking of migrating geese.

When the activity level at the Inn at the Pines Lodge dropped, Emily visited her son in New York. I drove her to the airport in Des Moines and held her hand until she boarded her plane. She made me promise to eat something besides canned soup, and I made her promise to come back. I reverted to working extra hours, reading mystery novels, and tinkering with my car. I had lived most of my adult life in this manner, but now I felt lonely.

***

I received a photo mailer from Oklahoma a week after Emily left. It contained several photos and a letter from Ms. Leighton explaining that the work had progressed faster than she had expected and the photos were of the facial masks over the casts. She noted that the wigs on the masks were fashioned to match the hair samples of each owner and styled according to the period. She emphasized that several of the features on the masks were guess work and that latex masks could be made from the clay and putty models.

I laid the photos on my coffee table; there were four for each mask: a frontal view, right and left profiles, and a three-quarter view. Finally, I thought, I was looking at people, but exceptionally regular people. The reconstruction of the flesh, as Ms. Leighton had warned, did yield a face, but not an individual face. Unique markings such as scars, pits, dimples, freckles, or wrinkles, could not be reproduced. I had the faces of six mannequins. But that was better than six skulls.

I spent my lunch break the next day convincing Ervin to print the pictures and the descriptions of their owners in the *Reporter*. I had to talk to Ervin at a desk labeled LOCAL NEWS. He excused himself, donned his green eye shade, and rummaged among his printing equipment. He returned without the shade and announced that there was room for the pictures and the story on page two. I made him promise to exclude any allusions to devil worship in the article.

The *Reporter* carried the story when it was delivered Thursday afternoon. The *Des Moines Register* picked it up in its Fri-

day edition, and WHO, which may have been trying to atone
for the actions of Scott Christen, devoted five minutes of its
Saturday evening news cast to the mysterious skeletons of
Bishop County. The coverage was much more than I had expected, and I was certain that someone would recognize at
least one picture or description.

Bird banged on my garage door Sunday morning. "Bill,
you out here?"

"Yeah, Bird. What do you need?" I was underneath my
Mercury.

"Nothing. Just coming around. What you doing?"

"Right now, putting on some new tie rods. Later, I'm going to see if I can get the A-arms off so the machine shop can
press in some new bushings."

Bird made a seat out of a box full of old magazines.
"Sounds like a lot of work."

"Yeah. But it needs to be done, and I don't have much else
to do."

"Yeah. Lots of coverage on those skeletons all of a sudden.
You behind that?"

I grunted as I freed a worn tie rod. "I had the faces recon-
structed by a lady in Oklahoma, and I gave the story to Ervin.
It mushroomed on its own from there."

"Didn't say nothing to me about it."

I scooted from under the car. "Wasn't anything to say. I
didn't know if the faces would come out, and I certainly didn't
plan this kind of coverage. Besides, you told me that you
weren't interested and that I could investigate all I wanted."

"That's right, I did. And I'm still not interested unless you
got something. Did you?"

"Not a damned word. Televised over most of Iowa and

not a single word." I sighed. "I guess it's like you said: too much time has passed."

"Tried to tell you that a few times. If, by some fluke, you get something solid, let me know. Don't look good for the sheriff to be in the dark. When's Emily coming home?"

"Couple more weeks," I said. "I really miss her. I didn't think I would since I'm used to being alone, but I do."

"Starting to be like a normal person. When she gets back, you two come over for dinner sometime. See how married people live." He unfolded himself from the box. "Tell me if you find out anything."

CHAPTER SIXTEEN

Annie visited me in the ER Tuesday morning, though I didn't recognize her at first. The last time I had seen her she was dressed in skimpy shorts and a halter top and pretended to be Paul's wife. She looked different in a turtle neck sweater and a mid-length skirt.

"That you under all those clothes, Annie?" I asked.

"Cool this morning, Doc. We could have an early frost."

"Wouldn't doubt it. Most of the leaves are down. Problem, Annie?"

"No, but I need to talk to you in private."

Although the ER was empty, I led Annie to my office. She settled into its single, straight-back chair and laid a copy of the *Reporter* on my desk.

"I can't be sure, Doc, but I think this picture of the last lady could be my great-great aunt. The picture has the coloring all wrong. She was much lighter. Probably couldn't pass, but lighter than this." She poked her finger at the image in the paper.

"The coloring was just a guess," I said. "Her skeleton had

features that suggested she was black and corresponding characteristics were used to reconstruct her face. What about the description? Was your aunt a big woman?"

"I think so. I never saw her, of course, but my grandmother took care of me when I was little, and she used to show me pictures and tell me stories about the people in her family album. There was a picture of her mother and her sister, who would be my great-grandmother and great-great aunt. They were standing by a tree in a yard with a little girl, who was my grandmother, sitting on a tricycle in front of them. Everyone was smiling and looked happy. Anyway, my grandmother said that shortly after that picture was taken my great-great aunt disappeared. Taken by evil men, my grandmother said. It upset my great-grandmother, because my grandmother said she never smiled like in the picture again, and that she died a few years later of a broken heart." Annie looked at the floor. "Maybe it's just a story you tell a little kid, but I thought it might help."

"Annie," I asked, "did your great-great aunt ever live in Louisiana?"

She shrugged. "I don't know."

"Did your great-grandmother or grandmother live around Jackson County?"

"Yeah, most of my mother's family lived in Jackson. Some lived in Perry. Still do. How did you know that?"

"It fits in with an old newspaper story about a lady who disappeared who could have been your great-great aunt. Do you know her name?"

"No. I'm sure that my grandmother said it a hundred times, but I can't remember. Maybe it was something like Edna or Ethyl. I tried all weekend to remember."

"Is your grandmother still alive?" I asked.

"No. She died when I was fifteen. I sort of ran away from home then."

"Well, Annie, it would be my guess that this lady," I tapped the picture, "is your great-great aunt."

"What happened to her, Doc?"

I sighed. This was too much like telling a relative bad news about a patient, which was one of the reasons I had avoided private practice. "I don't really know, Annie. It's almost impossible to determine the cause of death from a skeleton." I cleared my throat. "I don't think it was very pleasant, though. If it means anything, I think she fought like a tiger all the way to the end."

Annie gave a half smile. "It means something, I guess. I don't know why I feel so sad about this. I never knew her." Two tears glistened on her cheeks, and I offered her a box of tissues. She cried quietly with her shoulders shaking under her sweater.

"I'm sorry, Doc," she said after a final shudder. "I didn't intend to do this."

"Don't worry about it," I said. We sat silently a few minutes with the only sound being crumbling cellophane as I unwrapped a cigar.

"Would you like the remains?" I finally asked.

"Remains?"

"The remains of your aunt. Would you like me to release them to you? I thought if she had a marker or something you could bury them."

"Oh, I understand. Yes, I would, but I don't know anything about a marker. I'll try to find out. Can I wait?"

"Sure. Take all the time you need and thanks for coming in. You're the first big break in this mystery," I said.

"I'm glad it helped. Thanks for listening, Doc. " She smiled and stood up. "See you."

"Annie, you still doing tricks?" I asked before she left my office.

She shrugged. "Sort of. Business is slow now that tourist season's ended. Mostly we get drunks from the Golden Eagle on Friday night."

"Sounds romantic."

She laughed. "I wish."

"Why don't you do something else?"

She shrugged again. "Don't know much else. Started this when I ran away. Girl's got to eat, you know."

"Yeah, I know, but look for something else to do. You're young and pretty, and I don't want to see you old and ugly ten years from now. Or dead." I added.

I saw her shoulders tense under her sweater, and I figured that she would tell me to mind my own business. Her shoulders relaxed. "Thanks for caring," she said and left.

What I thought was a big break didn't impress Bird.

"Maybe you got one identified, if that hooker can remember her great-great aunt's name. Maybe she was from Louisiana and did disappear in nineteen thirty-one. Anybody see her abducted, go into the hotel, get killed? And what about the others? They all abducted together, separately, earlier, later? They all from Jackson County?"

"I guess it's not very much," I said, dejected.

"Hey," Bird slapped me on the back. "It's more than I ever thought we'd find out. At least one of the poor devils might get a decent burial."

***

Emily had given me a key so that I could water her plants,

which I did faithfully three times a week. She had entrusted Pansy to her neighbor, which relieved me of daily feedings. On watering days I sat at the table by the window and watched the world darken as I sipped brandy. I called Emily frequently, and she sent letters and postcards, but I missed the pats on my arm and the soft perfume of her hair. On other evenings I worked late, ate one of Emma's sandwiches, and read and drank brandy until I fell asleep in my recliner. Occasionally, I tried to figure out why Emily had affected me and why I seemed to have affected her. Our relationship had taken minimal effort to start, and we enjoyed each other's company. My marriage, my only other serious relationship, had been punctuated with volatile fights, vocal disagreements, and more than one separation. I had believed that love was accompanied by such unpleasant side effects, and wishing to avoid them, I avoided love. There had not been any of those unpleasant side effects in my relationship with Emily; maybe this was the first time I had actually known love.

***

An ambulance brought an elderly woman with chest pains to the ER on one of my late evenings. I had been alerted about her condition by the ambulance driver and had the crash cart and cardiac unit standing by. I had my stethoscope to her chest as soon as the gurney stopped. I heard a strong, steady, although somewhat rapid, heartbeat. Puzzled, I took her pulse. It, too, was strong and regular.

"Where is the pain exactly?" I asked.

"Here," the lady pointed. "It's going to kill me." Her face contorted, and she grit her teeth. "God help me."

"Ma'am, I want you to stand up."

"Can't," she said through locked teeth. "Ankle's broken."

I pulled the sheet back and saw a foot cast. "Then sit up. Give me your arms. I'll help."

I pulled one arm gently and guided her legs off the gurney. She grabbed my neck and tugged herself up. "My God, it hurts."

"I know it does. Hold on, I've got you." Her fingers dug into my neck as pain spasmed through her. I flinched; she had a strong grip.

"You feel a little better, now?" I asked after a minute.

"Pain's a little less," she said, catching her breath.

"Good. Don't lie back down. I'm going to help you into this wheelchair." I motioned to a nurse to bring a chair.

"Keep sitting as straight as you can," I instructed. "I know that you feel like doubling into the pain, but don't. It'll make it worse. I'm going to take another listen." I pressed my stethoscope to several places on her abdomen and heard the rumbling of Vesuvius each time.

"What did you have for dinner, ma'am?"

"Beef stroganoff, broccoli, cucumber salad, and some pecan pie."

I shook my head. The old gal could eat, and that could do it. I told the nurse to get some antacid and tell the cardiac unit to stand down.

"A couple of swigs of this will make you feel better in a bit," I said and tipped the medicine into her mouth.

Within a minute her breathing became more regular. "It's better," she said. "Not gone, but better. What was wrong with me? Did I have a heart attack?"

"Acute gastritis." I said.

"What's that in English?"

"Gas."

"What? Gas did this? I've had gas before, young man, and it wasn't like this."

"No, ma'am, I'm sure it wasn't. Your gas was severe this time, and I suspect that you have a hiatal hernia. When the gas pushes on that, it's very painful and can feel like a heart attack."

"Well, I'll be, " she said, visibly relieved. "Just gas?"

"I think you may be constipated, too, which made the gas so severe this time," I said.

She waved her hand at her foot. "I haven't been right since I broke that ankle last week."

"You might try a lighter diet, more fruit and roughage. Maybe a laxative. Stay away from stroganoff and pecan pie for awhile. Use any antacid from the drug store at the first hint of indigestion. Now, I'm going to admit you for tonight and have your regular doctor check you out tomorrow, just in case. But I'm pretty sure that will take care of it. Someone come with you?"

"My daughter rode in the ambulance with me."

"Fine. I'll have the nurse take her to admitting to get you set up, and you can help me fill out these forms for the ER." I retrieved the forms from the nurses' station. "Okay. Name?"

"Janet Stolmyer. S-T-O-L-M-Y-E-R."

"How old are you Mrs. Stolmyer?"

"Eighty-seven."

"Eighty-seven?" I was astonished. "I thought you were in your sixties."

She smoothed her white hair. "People say that. I've been lucky. Hardly ever sick, always active. At least until I broke this stupid ankle."

"How'd you do that?" I asked.

"Stepped in a blamed mole hole when I was gardening. I'd like to step on that little squirt's head. Have to get around in a wheel chair, and I don't like it one bit."

I squatted and looked at the cast. "Mrs. Stolmyer, you might ask your doctor about a walking cast. You know, those kind with a rubber stopper on the bottom. You could probably get around with a cane then, if you took it easy. Might help your digestion, too."

"I'll try anything to get out of this chair. I'm sick of cards and daytime television. I want to do something. Thank you, Doctor—" she read my name tag, "Mullins. I'll ask him tomorrow when he sees me."

"You may not qualify for one. I didn't set your ankle, but it can't hurt to ask."

"It sure can't," she said. "Say, you're not George Mullins' boy, are you?"

"Yes."

"Thought you moved away?"

"I did. I moved back a few years ago after my father passed."

"Oh. He used to fix my car. Good mechanic."

"Yes, he was."

"I've seen your name in the paper. You're trying to find out about those skeletons from that old hotel, aren't you?"

"Yeah. Haven't had much luck, though."

She sat silently for a moment then said softly, "I think the Klan might have something to do with them."

"Klan?"

"The Ku Klux Klan. They were powerful around that time. Still pretty powerful today, from what I understand."

"Oh, okay." I figured that Mrs. Stolmyer must be related to Ervin Johnston.

"Don't treat me like a doddering old woman," she snapped. "I'm in full possession of my faculties."

"But the Klan? In Bishop? That's something that was in the south a long time ago. Not here in Bishop. Not now."

She cocked her head and regarded me. "You don't know? No one has approached you?"

I shook my head.

"I guess you did move away when you were young. Maybe they figured you were a liberal since you lived in California. Your father never told you?"

I shook my head again.

"Well, he never belonged. Too good a man. My Harvey didn't either. I'd have kicked his butt from here to Des Moines if he even thought about joining those idiots." She shook her fist in the air. "You really never knew?"

"No," I found my voice. "But please tell me."

"Well," she shifted in her chair, "might as well start at the beginning. I first learned about the Klan when I was eighteen. I had just married my Harvey, and we had a farm next to the Atherton place. That was their meeting place. From our bedroom window, we could see them dancing in their sheets around burning crosses. Lots of tom foolery, that's what Harvey and I thought, and we made fun of them from our window. Then the depression hit, and people lost their jobs, homes, farms, everything. Lots of them hit the road to find any type of work. Some hitched on the highways; others rode the freight trains. I guess you wouldn't know it now since all the tracks are gone, but Bishop was a junction for a railroad line that ran from Omaha. At Bishop it split; one track headed to Chicago, and the other to Minneapolis. Mostly used to ship cattle to the stockyards. Some of the people that rode the trains started camping by the tracks outside of town. Some would hop a train out, and others would come in. Nobody in town was very happy about it, and Harvey told me that there was talk about burning them out, but it was just talk. Then Mr. Atherton died. I can't remember his first name, but his son, Noah, who was just a bit older than I was, whipped those members into frenzies. Crosses burning every night, dancing and chanting. More and more members. They burned out that tent city one night. After that, the Klan was a big hero. Got rid of all those hoboes. Sheriff joined, and so did the mayor. Didn't anyone dare speak against them. They just took over Bishop. That became the Klan's job in Bishop. Keep out any drifters, hoboes, and anyone undesirable. I hate to think how they did that, but I don't think it was pleasant."

"Jesus Christ Almighty," I said.

"You said it. I understand it's pretty much the same today."

"Today? Come on."

"Keep up on the news, Doctor. There's been a resurgence. They've cast off their sheets and call themselves the New Klan. Portray themselves as crusaders for the white working class. Some have even run for office. But they're the same fools that danced around crosses."

"But in Bishop?"

"Still have the same job. Keep out the undesirables. Give us a nice, clean, safe town. 'Course, you know who the undesirables are: anyone that's not white and Christian. You ever see anyone in Bishop that wasn't?"

"No, I guess not." When I returned from Los Angeles, I was struck that everyone in Bishop looked alike. Differences existed in hair and eye color, but never skin color. Even the tourists were white.

"These Athertons," I asked, "what happened to them?"

"I haven't seen Noah in years. I heard he had a stroke. I see his sons at church sometimes. Far as I know they still farm the same land. Why? You going to try to do something?"

"I don't know. Try to find out what I can, I guess."

"You'll make this old lady's soul rest easier."

She was silent again for a few moments. I had turned off the examining lights and in the softer lights that filtered in from the hallway her face aged and lost its self-assurance.

"There's something else you should know," she continued in a voice barely above a whisper. I moved closer to her chair. "I hate to speak of it; it shames me so." She sighed deeply and wiped her eyes.

"My husband, Harvey, was born in Texas. When he was quite young his father died. The neighbor family had a boy, I think his name was John, who was about eight or ten years older than Harvey, and he became his big brother. And kind of a surrogate father, I suppose. Anyway, he taught him the things a man teaches a boy; you know, how to hunt and fish, ride a horse, and I guess, about girls. When Harvey was fourteen or fifteen, he and his mother moved to Iowa, but he and John corresponded several times a year. John worked on a ranch and eventually became foreman or manager, or whatever it's called. The depression hit that part of Texas hard, what with the drought and all. John wrote that the ranch was failing and he'd soon be out of a job and a place to live. Naturally, Harvey invited him to stay with us. In his last letter John accepted, said he was coming north, and would try to find work on his way to Iowa. He figured he might arrive in Bishop by early fall.

"Harvey was delighted, but I was worried. You see, John was black. Harvey said he had Indian blood in him, but in the picture I saw of him, he was black. I urged Harvey to tell him not to come because of the Klan, but he insisted that John could take care of himself, and could probably show those Klansmen a thing or two. He had quite an inflated idea of John. Big brother worship, I suppose.

"We never saw or heard from John again. I honestly don't know what happened to him, but I have a terrible suspicion that I've kept buried for seventy-five years. The night the Klan burned out the camp they had a huge meeting at the Atherton place. They whooped and hollered until all hours. Bunch of drunken no accounts. Kept Harvey and me up most of the night. Even when they left to do their burning and it was quiet, we didn't sleep much what with being angry, worried, and scared.

"Harvey left early that morning to work the field on the other side of our farm. I cleaned up after breakfast, but I was tired and I went upstairs to lie down. Wasn't long and I heard a commotion at Atherton's. I saw them leading people that were tied up into the barn. I don't know what went on inside, but it couldn't have been good. Later, I saw Noah and another fellow load all of them, five or six, I guess, onto his truck and drive away. I never saw any of those people again.

"One of the men could have been Harvey's friend. I was too far away to see faces, and I'd never met John, but I know that two black men and a black woman were led into the barn. I remember a couple of other women, too, but I don't think that they were black. I told Harvey about it that evening. We talked about what to do for hours, days, in fact. But what could we do? The sheriff, the mayor, and half the town be-longed to the Klan, and most were at Atherton's that night. Who could we tell? And what with the Klan growing, and the meetings becoming more and more frequent with more and more people, Harvey and I became afraid and hid our guilt. We convinced ourselves that nothing really happened. That maybe Noah just gave those people a ride to the county line or some such thing. We figure that John found work and started a new life somewhere else."

She stopped, focused her eyes on me and asked "He probably was one of those poor people, wasn't he?"

It took me a moment to realize she was asking me a question. "Uh, well," I stammered, trying to collect my thoughts. "Two of the skeletons were of black men, and one did ride a horse. There were ridges on his leg bones that indicated that. I'd have to look at the report again to give you the exact terms. He was in his late twenties or early thirties when he died. Would that be right?"

"Harvey was twenty-two then, and John was ten years older— thirty-two. That does fit. Do you know anything else?"

"Just that someone whacked him a good one on the back of the head. That's what killed him."

"It was him. I'm sure now. I think I was sure the day I saw Noah Atherton lead him into that barn, but I didn't want to admit it."

"Let me get this straight. You saw these people? You're a witness?"

"Well, I guess so. I never saw what happened to them, though."

"But you saw them tied up and forced into a barn?"

"Yes, but I don't know what good that does."

"I'm not sure I do either, but it's better than nothing, and it's a place to start."

She smiled, and the years fell off her face. "I do feel much better, Doctor."

**

After work the next day, I stopped at the post office and got directions to the Atherton farm. It was south of town where the land folded into gentle hills and valleys around Goose Creek, a tributary of the Des Moines River. I found the Atherton homestead quickly; it rested in a large valley and the house sat a few hundred yards off the county road. But I knew it couldn't have been the place that Mrs. Stolmyer remembered. The house was new, no more than five years old, and the poplars and spruce that had been planted for a windbreak were just getting size and were years from maturity. The barn and outbuildings looked older, but they had certainly been built after the 'thirties. Yet the mailbox clearly read "Atherton," and I had followed the directions exactly.

I pulled to the shoulder and considered. Obviously the house that Mrs. Stolmyer remembered had been replaced, hardly an uncommon occurrence. Was this new house still the Klan headquarters? Were Noah Atherton's sons the leaders? Had the Klan vanished from Bishop like the old house? Did Mrs. Stolmyer have an overactive imagination? I watched cattle forage through the stalks of a harvested corn field, reached no answers, shoved the van in gear, and drove home.

The following afternoon I visited Mrs. Stolmyer's home. She lived in a nicely kept house that was loosely patterned after the Queen Anne style. Large shutters bordered three windows that faced the street, and two stone lions guarded the porch. Roses and geraniums lined the porch and walkway, but were dormant in the cool weather.

A middle-aged lady, whom I took to be Mrs. Stolmyer's daughter, answered my knock and led me into a parlor where Mrs. Stolmyer sat on a period love seat, with her foot resting on a matching foot stool.

"Why, Doctor, what a nice surprise. I must say you were right. My doctor pronounced my heart sound as a dollar and released me straight away. He said he'd see about a walking cast next week."

"That's great. Glad you feel better," I said. "I went by the Atherton place yesterday."

She motioned me to a chair across from her and looked into my eyes. "And?"

"And it's nothing like you remember. In fact, it's new. The house you remember must have been torn down."

"Oh, my. I suppose that's what happened. I guess that destroyed any clues."

"I suppose. I'm kind of at a loss for how to proceed. I can't very well knock on the door and ask if they belong to the Klan."

"No, of course not," she said. "I remember that house as if it were yesterday. It sat way off the road behind a hill. A lane wound around to it. I always thought it was funny that it was so far back from the road, but I guess it helped keep things secret."

"Wait a minute. The house I saw wasn't built anywhere like that. It was just a couple hundred yards from the road and in a big valley. You sure?"

"Positive," she nodded. "Our place was farther along and at the top of a hill. That's how we could see Atherton's."

"Weren't any hills close by this house. Suppose they built on a new location?"

"They must have. Where did you go exactly?"

"Down County Road Fifty-Eight about five miles south of town. House sits on the east side of the road."

"No, our place was farther east. Lots of farms changed hands in the 'seventies and 'eighties. Athertons probably bought up more land and built a new house."

"Yeah, I suspect that you're right, Mrs. Stolmyer," I continued. "I've got a county map in my van. Do you think you could find Atherton's old place on it?"

"I could try. Why? You think you might find something?"

"Well, if the house was that far from the road, it might have been easier just to let it sit instead of pulling it down."

"Good point. Let's look."

CHAPTER SEVENTEEN

I left work early the next day and followed Ms. Stolmyer's directions until I ended up on a dirt road that was no more than a path, hopelessly lost and wondering if the Atherton house had only been a product of an old lady's mind. I was looking for a place wide enough to turn around when I saw a gate with "Tarnish" in paint-dripped, hand-lettering on the top board. The gate wasn't locked, and I drove a few hundred yards beyond it to the Tarnish homestead, which consisted of a collapsed barn, a clapboard house with sheets of plastic insulating the windows, and tangles of wire, pipes, and car parts strewn in the yard. Lou was in the rear of the house chopping wood.

"Hey, Lou," I called. "It's Doc Mullins."

Lou set down his ax. "Well, howdy-do, Doc. Weren't expecting nobody. Something wrong?" He ejected a stream of tobacco juice.

I walked closer. "Tell the truth, Lou, I'm lost. I was trying to find the old Atherton place."

Lou snorted, "No wonder you're lost. Ain't been nobody

there for years. Since Noah went to the nursing home. Road's all
growed over. His kids didn't want it. Too old, I suppose. Built
theirselves a new, modern one on the other side of the farm.
Good house just going to waste." He expelled some more juice
and wiped his chin. "I been sneaking a little pipe out of it, though.
No sense in that going to waste. What you want it for?"

"Uh, I was thinking of buying it and wanted to see it."

Lou grunted. "You'll need a light. Pretty dark in there.
Follow that path by the creek. It's just over that rise." He
gestured with a grimy flashlight that he had extracted from
his rear pocket.

I accepted the light and walked toward the creek.

"Hey, Doc," Lou called behind me. "You ain't going to
hold that pipe against me? Didn't know anyone was interested
in the place."

"No, Lou, it's all right," I called back just as I found the path.

The Atherton house was a perfectly square two-story building adorned with a front porch and a cupola at its roof's crest.
Several of its windows were boarded and a hole gaped in the
roof. The yard where the Klansmen once danced, chanted,
and tortured was overgrown with weeds and small cedar trees.
A blue jay squawked a warning from its nest under a beam on
the porch. He flapped angrily to a cedar tree, still squawking,
as I tried the front door. It was locked or stuck, and I walked
around back. The jay's protests ceased when I disappeared
from his nesting area. The back door yielded with a shove,
and I found myself in the kitchen. Lou was right; it was dark,
and I switched on the flashlight and grinned. Lou had taken
the fixtures besides a little pipe, and a jagged hole marked the
kitchen sink's former location. I picked my way through the
rooms. Each was empty. Lou had removed the bathroom fix-

tures as well, except for crumbs of rotten plaster and the stench of mildew. I climbed the ladder to the attic, and the eyes of an opossum family reflected my beam. I retreated to fresh air. No torture chambers, no hooded sheets, no crosses. Whatever crimes and indecencies had happened here now existed only in an old lady's mind and in the silent walls of the deteriorating house.

***

On Saturday a cold rain kept me in my recliner with a new mystery. I was unable to focus my attention and set it aside to consider my own mystery. I had to admit that I was not nearly as successful as the fictional detectives I had read about for years. I still had no idea who most of the skeletons once were or what had happened to them in the old hotel. I had learned only that the Klan was active in Bishop during the 'thirties and that Noah Atherton headed it. However, I realized, I knew this only through an old woman whose memory may have faded. Atherton's house revealed only that Lou Tarnish was a quintessential scavenger. I left my chair and watched the rain drops hit the puddles in the street. I decided that since the past was inscrutable, I'd try the present. Mrs. Stolmyer said that the Klan still provided a safe, clean community, so there must be active members somewhere in Bishop. I watched the rain turn to drizzle and decided that the Golden Eagle would be as good a place as any to start looking.

When I pushed open the black and gold door of the bar I was immediately disappointed that its members were not wearing sheets and hoods and a cross wasn't burning behind the bar. When my eyes adjusted I saw ten pairs of eyes regarding me suspiciously. I recognized most of the patrons, but didn't know their names. I knew some of them recognized me, too, but I had never been in this bar, and I had invaded their sanctum. I ordered a brandy, which only emphasized that I was a foreigner. I was informed that the Golden Eagle's stock was limited to bourbon, scotch, vodka, gin, and beer. I ordered a beer and looked at surroundings that were replicated in thousands of bars across the country—a couple of pool tables, a pinball machine, a dart board, and a television tuned to a football game. Its attempt at individuality was a stuffed eagle with wings covered with dust that sat on a shelf above the cash register. I feigned interest in the game and listened to the conversation, hoping to hear something about the Klan. I didn't; talk was limited to the game, and, by the fourth quarter, my strangeness had worn off, and I was included. I contributed some innocuous generalizations, and, when the game concluded was thought to be regular enough to be invited to play pool. I shot a couple of games, lost both, and returned to the bar to join in a conversation about the crappy weather. When the topic turned to the government and politics, I was sure that my quest would be rewarded. It wasn't. Although my new comrades and I took turns buying each other drinks for the next three hours, I learned only that beer makes me nauseous, I wasn't a good pool player, and the working class think that they are being ripped off by high taxes and corrupt politicians. I gathered not the slightest hint about Klan members or activities. I went home discouraged and depressed.

I didn't feel much better the next morning. I missed Emily and Paul, and the weather was again cold and gray. I settled into my recliner with the Sunday paper. I had read the comics and glanced through the *Parade Magazine* when I realized that the *Des Moines Register* had reported the news for Iowa for generations. If any activities of Bishop's Klan were made public or there was an investigation into it, the *Register* would have reported it. I made arrangements to miss work on Monday, packed a change of clothes, and drove to Des Moines.

I was at the *Register's* offices when they opened, and I followed the directory to the archives on the third floor where I faced a long counter, behind which were several computer terminals and microfilm readers. The *Register* had long since abandoned Ervin Johnston's method of recording. A lady in her early twenties was busily punching the keyboards on one of the computers. She was intent in her work and didn't notice me for several moments.

"Oh, I'm sorry. I didn't know anyone was here. No one usually comes in this early. Just a minute and I'll be with you."

Her fingers tapped some more keys; she rose from the chair, smoothed her skirt and hair, donned a pair of wire-rimmed glasses and approached the counter. She was tall and lanky with a broad face and did little to enhance her appearance: her hair hung limply on either side of her face; she wore no make-up; her blouse and skirt were utilitarian.

"I'm Ms. Ravenwoods," she said. "How can I help you?"

I explained what I wanted; she nodded and powered another computer and began punching keys. "We have almost every topic cross-filed in the network now," she explained as she waited for the program to load. "For each topic the computer will list any articles or references by date. I'll know if we have anything in a minute."

She sat behind the screen and removed her glasses. "I don't see anything on the Klan in the 'thirties or 'forties, but there are a couple of feature stories on it in the 'fifties and 'sixties. Do you want those?"

I nodded, and she printed the dates and issue numbers of

the papers. She showed me how to locate the issues in the microfilm files and how to load the reader. I thanked her and squinted at the screen. I read every word of the articles, four in all, and found nothing on any activities in Iowa. Disappointed, I returned the reels to their shelves and prepared to leave.

"Find what you want?" Ms. Ravenwoods asked from behind the counter.

"No."

"Well. don't give up yet. Let's check some corresponding topics."

During the next three hours I read articles on local elections, political corruption, civil rights, fringe politics, and social groups. Ms. Ravenwoods proved an able archivist and searched for any possible articles in her computer and located their microfilm for me. In the early afternoon in an article on the changing political climate after World War II, I found what I wanted. A short paragraph noted that the politics of an unnamed central Iowa county had been controlled by an unnamed influential farmer for many years. It was suspected, the article said, that the farmer had ties to the Klan and ran the county accordingly. I was certain the county was Bishop and the farmer was Noah Atherton. I had Ms. Ravenwoods make me copies, thanked her for her help, and, on impulse, asked her to lunch. Her eyes sparked, the spark became a question, then confusion. She declined and returned to the safety of her computers.

On my way home my mood alternated between delight that I had verified Mrs. Stolmyer's story and frustration that I couldn't learn more. Every path I took seemed blocked, and I wondered if I ever would know what happened to those six people. I recalled Doctor Learner saying that a man needs a challenge. I had certainly picked a big enough one, I thought, as I crossed into Bishop County.

On a whim, and to avoid sitting alone in my house, I drove to Atherton's old house. I vaguely hoped the house might give me some new ideas.

I borrowed Lou's flashlight again, telling him I needed to check a couple of things before I decided whether to buy or not. He reiterated that it would be good to have neighbors and apologized about the pipe.

The house was absolutely unchanged. The same weeds and cedar trees grew around it; the same jay nested on the porch, and the rooms held the same gaping holes where Lou had removed fixtures and pipe. It stood oblivious to time and hid its past. I shone my light into every corner, but the house refused to release its secret. I sighed and went out into the fresh air.

I was watching some crows pick in a field below the house among the corn stalks for any kernel missed in harvesting and was resigning myself to another dead end, probably the final one, when the earth beneath my left foot gave way and my leg dangled into a void. I jerked my leg out, banged my shin, and shone my light into the hole. Pale crickets hopped from the light, and I saw a broken board on a brick floor about six feet below. A root cellar, I thought. I remembered my father telling me that he played in his father's in the summer because it was cool. I pulled back the rest of the rotted boards and saw a steep, brick stairway. I figured I had just as well go all the way, and I descended, holding the walls for balance. Beetles and centipedes scurried from my light. The air was cool, but pungent from the wet earth, and I took short breaths through my mouth. A couple of forgotten jars of canned food had erupted their putrid contents onto the shelves, providing food for the subterranean insects. A broken crock littered the floor and half-covered a metal box. I grabbed the box, disturbing a score of cinch bugs, and stumbled to daylight. I lay on the grass gagging and coughing out the cellar's fetid air.

When my breathing became regular I examined the box. It was the size of a tool chest, constructed of stout metal, and secured with an equally stout padlock. It was heavy, and I had to switch carrying arms several times as I teetered down the path to the Tarnish place. I secured the box in my van and returned the flashlight to Lou.

"What you think, Doc? Going to buy it?" Lou was scraping mud from his boots on the back step. "Be nice to have a neighbor. Missus wants to know if you want to stay to dinner."

"Thanks, Lou, but I got to get back to the hospital," I prudently declined.

Lou extracted a mass of tobacco and hurled it into the weeds. "Well, maybe next time. See you."

I saw them stacked by the side of the house. I picked up the top one. It was made completely of sticks shaped into a small lattice.

"Hey, Lou," I called to him before he shut the door. "Where'd you get these?"

"Those damn things," he said. "Come out of Atherton's attic. Thought I could make rabbit pens out of them, but they're too damned flimsy. Just saving them for kindling. Take a couple if you want."

***

In my garage, I broke the padlock with a tire iron and a sledge hammer. The top layer consisted of several papers containing lists of names, some typed and some hand-written. I rifled past those, saw an announcement for a Klan rally dated 1959, came to a handbook with the single word "Bylaws" on the cover, and found them. Handbills with poorly reproduced, but unmistakably, pictures of the permanent occupants of the hotel.

The top bill showed the pair from the first room, the black man and the Indian woman posed in a doggie-style sex position. The man's head lolled to the side and his arm dangled. The woman's face was hidden, and she was propped at an unnatural angle. They were dead. The bill's banner proclaimed, "The Klan Keeps Perverts Out of Bishop."

The second bill displayed the black man and white woman from the second room with the man smothering the woman in the missionary position. Its banner read, "The Klan Stops Sex Crazed Nigger Rapists."

The last bill showed the black woman, Annie's great-great aunt, and the white pregnant girl above the banner, "The Klan Handles Nigger Sex Perverts."

The box contained several copies of each handbill and underneath them were the original photos. I had been right; several pictures of the victims had been taken in various positions, possibly for other handbills. All the pictures displayed the victims nearly nude and in sexual positions. The black man from the first room was in a torn cotton shirt, the Indian woman had the disheveled remnants of a skirt or slip around her waist, and the pregnant girl had a nightie shoved above her breasts, which accounted for the cotton and silk fibers that Doctor Learner found.

The handbills were the Klan's propaganda, which justified its existence, advertised its power, and spread its hate to gullible people. Six people and a fetus sacrificed their lives for that propaganda. Bile rose in my throat and my mouth dried. I puked on the way to the house.

I forced down some soup and crackers and a large glass of brandy and investigated the box further. The lists were yearly roster sheets of whom I assumed were Klan members. The rosters were in reverse order in the box starting with 1985 on the top and ending with 1931 on the bottom. I remembered that Mrs. Stolmyer said that Noah Atherton had inherited the Klan leadership in the early 'thirties. Apparently, I was looking at Noah's comrades in his fifty-four year reign of terror. I scanned the 1985 roster; sixty-seven total names with, I did a double take to confirm it, Mayor Michael Ellerbrock's name on the front sheet. "Never liked him much," I muttered and flipped to the second page. Blood rushed in my ears, and my eyes locked on the name "Casper Schmidt."

"Eugene Starling"appeared directly below it.

"Jesus, Mary, and Joseph," I repeated several times when I had breath. I pressed my head to the back of my chair and clamped my eyes shut. The thoughts, "I was wrong," and "Eyes played a trick on me," and "Not a roster of Klan members," flashed on my lids like chairs on a Ferris wheel. I looked again. It *was* a roster of Klan members, and the names *were* there. I knew how Mrs. Stolmyer felt sixty years ago. What do you do and who do you tell when you're the only one on the outside?

A horrifying thought struck me. I grabbed the list and searched for "Harden." There wasn't any. I checked all the rosters back to 1970. I wasn't completely alone.

***

I put the rosters, handbills, and photos into two file folders and slipped them into my file drawer in my office before I started my shift. I opened the drawer a couple of times half expecting the images of the six skeletons to burst forth. Satis-

fied that the files looked innocuous, I reported to the ER. On
my lunch break I carried the folders to the doctors' lounge
and made copies. Twice someone entered the lounge, and I
was certain the pages would shout their horrors. I kept my
head down and projected interest in my work, and I was ig-
nored. I replaced the originals with the copies in my file drawer
and was then at a loss. I'd made the copies instinctively, probably from reading mystery novels, but now had no idea what
to do with them. Logically, the originals should be kept in the
file drawer, or any other safe place, and the copies should be
entrusted to a reliable person for safe keeping. But who could
I trust? Probably most people in town were in the Klan or
knew someone who was. Paul? Emily? I didn't want either of
them in danger. Where did the characters in the novels put
stuff for safe keeping? Their lawyers, I thought. They gave
their secrets to their lawyers with instructions that if anything
happened to them the secrets would be released. I should send
the copies to my lawyer. Except I didn't have a lawyer. But I
did know the lawyer that probated my father's estate. Maybe
he could help me. His name was probably at home with the
reams of paper that it took to end my father's life. He lived in
Des Moines, and was likely untouched by Bishop's Klan.

I spent the final hours of my shift mentally developing
those instructions and decided that in the event that any harm
came to me a copy of the box's contents should go to the
media, a second copy to the NAACP lawyer who I had read in
Time had successfully prosecuted racist organizations like the
Klan, and the originals to Paul. I figured he should know
something about Casper Schmidt if I were unable to explain
it to him. That thought crystallized my mortality, and I realized that I was beginning something dangerous with permanent consequences.

My lawyer informed me that the arrangement was as simple as providing him with the location of the documents and giving him the power of attorney. He said he could have the paperwork ready for my signatures the following afternoon. I transferred the file folders to my newly rented safe deposit box during my lunch break the following day, and I drove to Des Moines after work and signed the papers before my lawyer left for the day. That evening I felt safer sitting in my recliner sipping brandy and considering my next move.

CHAPTER EIGHTEEN

A hard frost greeted Bishop Saturday morning. Windows were laced with intricate designs, and the yards were white with ice crystals clinging to dead grass. As I made breakfast the radio announcer pondered the effects of an early winter on next year's corn crop.

Bird was putting storm windows on his second story windows when I pulled into his drive.

"Hey, Bill. Just in time to help," he called from the ladder. "Been busy and didn't get this done. Winter caught me by surprise."

"You and a lot of people," I said, realizing that my windows still held screens. After twenty years in California preparing for winter was not an easily reinstated habit. "I'll help, but I'm not climbing that ladder."

"No need. Just take the screen as I slide it down and push the storm window up. Save me a lot of climbing."

"I guess I can handle that," I said and reached for the screen.

Two hours later Bird and I warmed ourselves in his living room.

"Saved me a lot of time. I wanted to finish before Patty and the girls got back from Des Moines. Drove down early to get winter outfits for the girls. You by for any special reason, or you just killing time until Emily gets home? When's she coming anyway?"

"Tomorrow afternoon. I'm going to get her at the airport. And I came by to tell you that I know why the people in the hotel were killed."

"Damn, Bill. This is getting to be a real obsession with you. I don't think it's any too healthy. After all, they're just bones."

"Maybe so, but they were killed and posed for pictures. Sex pictures mostly. They were used for propaganda."

"Oh," Bird chuckled, "you're pretty sure about that? Who would want that type of propaganda?"

"The Klan."

Bird laughed outright. "The Klan? The Ku Klux Klan? What did they have to do with that old hotel?"

"I don't guess they had anything to do with the hotel. It was just a handy place to carry out their perversions and seal away the evidence."

"Yeah, could have been handy for anyone as much as it was empty. What made you decide the Klan did it?" Bird was still smiling.

"The Klan's been around Bishop for years, Bird. You know that. They had a real insurgence of new members in the 'thirties. Just about when those skeletons were sealed away."

Bird's smile faded. "How do you know about the Klan?"

"I've been doing some research and talking to people. Found out old man Atherton ran it."

"Who told you that?"

"Not important. But I did some more investigating and

found evidence that links the Klan to the murders of those six people."

"Well, I'll be damned," Bird said. "What evidence? Where is it? Is it enough to get an arrest warrant?"

"I'd say so, but I don't think that you'd want to," I said. "I found some other stuff, too."

"Yeah?" Bird's brows crooked in anticipation. "Well, shouldn't you turn it over to me and let me judge? Can't be withholding evidence."

"I'm the medical examiner, Bird. I can keep all the evidence I need to establish cause of death. And I won't be turning anything over to you."

"What?"

"I found the rosters of all the Klan members." I looked straight at the floor. "Your name was on the list, Bird."

I could feel Bird's eyes on me, but I stared at the floor. I was uncomfortably warm, and sweat dripped down my neck. Bird's mantle clock ticked off an eternity.

"You're bluffing. Just like you did with that reporter fellow. We looked Atherton's house up and down after he had his stroke. There's no records, and there's no pictures. You got squat," he snorted.

I took my eyes off the floor and looked into Bird's. He had been my best friend for almost my entire life. How could I know so little about him?

I cleared my throat forcefully. "Older houses, especially farm houses, had root cellars to store food. When the houses got electricity and refrigeration, the cellars were usually covered and forgotten. I found Atherton's."

Bird squeezed his eyes shut, and I felt myself being squeezed through his lids. "Damn that Noah Atherton. Secretive son of a bitch. Never told anyone where he hid his records. Then he up and has a stroke. Since nothing turned up after a few years we figured anything he had was gone for good. Leave it to you to muck things up." He sighed. "So what do you want?"

"First I want to know," I felt my anger rising, and I didn't check it, "I want to know why my best goddamn friend belongs to the goddamn Ku Klux Klan." I slammed the coffee table and felt my hand sting. "We grew up together, double dated in high school, and you got me my job when I came back home. Went around telling me to act right. Don't drink so much. Talk to your boy. Handle Maria. And all that time you're sneaking off in a goddamn white sheet burning goddamn crosses. You're a Klan member, Bird. A goddamn Klan member." I pushed a hot tear out of my eye and sank back to the couch. "My best friend is a son of a bitching Klan member," I sighed.

"We don't do that anymore." I heard Bird's voice in the distance. During my ranting he had moved across the room and propped himself against the mantel.

"Don't do what?" I asked, trying to regain my composure.

"Wear sheets and burn crosses. That was generations ago, in a different time and place. Actually, most members are just plain, hardworking men and women that want a fair chance at the American Dream. They don't like getting shut out of that dream by the government giving special privileges to a bunch of minorities that had nothing to do with building this country. We're a viable political force with a patriotic agenda—to protect the rights of the group the government wants to destroy—the white, Christian middle class. And we're doing a damned good job of it, too. We've got members elected to state legislatures, city councils, school boards, and the like.

Won't be long before we have representation in Washington. You think this is the only place that's run by the Klan? It's only one of many, many all over the country in every state. Actually, there are other organizations similar to the Klan— the Aryan Nations, Posse Comitatus, and Christian Identity. The Identity group has really been strong lately, and militias are becoming interested in our members. We're just getting bigger all the time. Couldn't expect us to be running around in sheets, now could you?"

I realized that I had expected in my search to recognize members by their sheets and hoods. Now I wondered if Bird's version of seemingly normal citizens leading lives of hate and racism was more frightening than the sheets.

"And I'll tell you what," I heard Bird continue. "Every town that has the Klan is better. Crime drops. No druggies or derelicts. Just good, reasonable, God-fearing people working for themselves and their families." Bird was resting his back against the mantle, and, with his arms and ankles crossed, he looked like a college professor delivering a lecture.

I shook off that image. "For chrissake, Bird. What is this drivel you're telling me? The Klan has been synonymous with torture, murder, lynching, and bombings for over a century. Good God, we learned that in history class twenty-five years ago. How can you believe that shit you're saying? What the hell is the matter with you?"

"I told you that was a different time and place. Not every political group started out pure. Democrats and Republicans had plenty of violence in their histories. Lord, America itself was founded on violence. Lots of religions had violent beginnings. It's necessary sometimes. It's not now, and we don't use it."

My head spun, and I thought I had gone through Alice's rabbit hole. Bird was portraying one of the most terrifying and horrifying organizations in America as a community service group and comparing it to the founding fathers and an instrument of God.

"Bird, you can't be serious. Christ, in high school we supported Martin Luther King. We made fun of all those ignorant segregationists. What happened to you? Who brainwashed you?"

"Nobody brainwashed me. I just saw reality. That civil rights stuff was fine then, but it went too far. Criminals have more rights than victims; special allowances are made for every group, money's given out to them helter skelter. All that takes away from the true Americans. You of all people ought to understand that, Bill."

"Me? What the hell are you talking about?"

"You've been to Los Angeles. You see what happens when you get masses of undesirables packed together. You get a bunch of drug addicts, gangsters, street walkers, pimps, pushers, and every other type of low life you can think of. The government goes broke trying to feed and clothe them. Shit, the jails are so full of that trash that dangerous criminals are turned loose. Hospitals can't take care of anybody else because they're so busy looking after people that are shot, overdosed, full of AIDS, and God knows what all. You can't tell me you didn't see that on your job every day. You're never going to see anything like that in Bishop. We'll see to that."

"Just how do you see to that? Kill them like those people in the hotel?"

"God, no. We just talk to them. Convince them they wouldn't be happy here. No violence. Nobody gets hurt. It's worked real good so far."

Bird was grinning down at me, clearly proud of his town
and pleased that he was winning this argument.

"Yeah, well, it isn't working that good. You missed a black
whore at the massage parlor. She's passing, but I figured that
experts like yourselves wouldn't be so easily fooled."

Bird's eyes narrowed for a second, and I knew that in my
desire to score a point, I had put Annie in some danger. I also
knew that I wasn't going to win. What humanity and reason
my friend had once possessed had been replaced with the
convoluted logic of a hate-monger.

"Tell me the truth, Bird. You already knew about the
skeletons in the hotel?"

"What? Hell, no. How could I? I wasn't even born then. I
doubt that the Klan had anything to do with it, despite what
you say."

"They sure as hell did."

"Just what makes you so sure? All you got is some bones."
Bird's chin protruded in a challenge.

I succumbed. "Noah took some pictures. I've got them.
Not the best quality, but certainly incriminating. I've also
got a witness."

"Bullcrap. Who?"

I bit my tongue to keep Mrs. Stolmyer's name from spill-
ing out. "I'm not saying. But I've got one."

"Hellfire, Bill, you're bluffing. That was sixty years ago.
Nobody remembers that far back. No evidence lasts that long.
You just got a bunch of guesses."

"Yeah, but I got damned good guesses. Maybe not enough to
stand up in court, but certainly good enough to interest the
media and the attorney general's office and probably several other
agencies. They might not think that a mayor and a sheriff belonging to the Klan is as good a thing as you think it is."

Bird cocked his chin again. "That what you're going to do? Go public?"

"I don't know what I'm going to do. But I'm going to do something. And I've got all the pictures and the other stuff hidden with a lawyer with instructions to release it to appropriate officials and media if anything happens to me."

Bird and I stared silently at each other. My friend of forty some years was gone. I'd never felt so alone.

I rose from the couch. "Bird, I'm going to call on some of the people on that list. You tell them it would be in their interest to be nice to me."

I stopped on the threshold with the open door in my hand. I looked back. "I'm sorry, Bird," I said. He kept staring at me with narrowed eyes. I closed the door.

I hit Bird's fence when I left his driveway, and I drove through Bishop to the amusement park unaware of anything beyond the asphalt in front of my van. Most of my past had been rewritten in the last twelve hours. Bishop, where I had learned to ride my bicycle, delivered newspapers, played baseball, had my first date, and buried my father had a core of hoods, crosses, torture, and death. My best friend, teammate, partner, and confidant, was at that core.

***

The massage parlor door displayed a closed sign, but I saw a light and a form moving behind its tinted glass. I banged on the door and got no response. I banged again and heard a muffled voice. I banged again.

"Look, read the sign," a voice shouted from directly behind the glass.

"I need to speak to Annie," I shouted back.

"Read the sign, asshole."

"It's important," I shouted again.

"Bug off."

"Hey, I'm the medical examiner for Bishop County. Open this damn door."

The door opened enough to reveal the red spiked hair, pimples, and dangling earrings of a man in his mid-twenties. "Got an ID?" he asked through the smoke from his cigarette.

I shoved my badge in his face. Ashes fell from his cigarette.

"So what do you want?" he asked.

"First thing I want is an apology. I don't like being called an asshole, you stupid dickhead. I want one fast or I'll close this place for health violations now and watch while your boss kicks your dumb ass." He didn't look bright enough to know the difference between a medical examiner and a health inspector.

"Yeah, okay, I'm sorry. But we get a lot of crazies hanging around, and you know—"

"Accepted," I said. "Now I need to see Annie. Official business," I added.

"She's not here."

"So where is she?"

"She lives in one of those little trailers in back of the snack bar. I don't know which one."

I found the trailers and was told by a blond in Spandex that Annie lived in the third one. By the time she answered the door in mussed hair and a cotton robe, I had little composure remaining and was certain Bird would appear over my shoulder at any moment.

"Annie, you've got to come with me right now."

"What's the matter, Doc?" she yawned. "Jeez, it's cold out. What time is it, anyway?"

"Doesn't matter. Look, Annie, I put you in some danger, and I want you to come with me."

"Danger? What are you talking about?"

I managed to push her out of the doorway, and I entered the trailer, which consisted of a single room with a fold-out bed, a sink, a hot plate, and a refrigerator. "Annie, I told the sheriff that you were black. Now, get some things together and come on."

"Black? So what? Not against the law to be black." Annie yawned and sat on the fold-out bed.

"It is in Bishop," I said. "Your great-great aunt was killed here in Bishop because she was black. She wasn't the only one."

Annie pushed the hair out of her face and put her dark eyes on mine. "You know that for a fact?"

I nodded. "Yes. And I think you are in some danger."

"Shit," she said, "let me get some stuff together."

I drove randomly through Jackson County, out of Bird's jurisdiction, as I told Annie about Mrs. Stolmyer's story, the Atherton house, the pictures and rosters in the box, and my conversation with Bird.

"Goddamn," she said when I finished. "Unbelievable. Just plain unbelievable."

"It's true," I said.

"The Klan right here," she laughed. "I bet half of those guys on that list screwed me. Boy, they'd be pissed to know they did it to a black girl."

"Irony is everywhere," I chuckled. "Do you have some relatives or friends that you can stay with?"

"Not really. Some cousins in Perry, but I haven't seen them in years."

"That's it?" I asked.

"Yeah. I told you that my grandmother raised me. My mother died when I was little, and when my grandmother died, I was put in a foster home. I hated it, and I ran away." She paused. "And now I'm here."

"Yeah, and what to do with you?" I wondered. "Can't stay in Bishop. Can't live in a motel room forever. If you knew someone who lived in Jackson County—" I realized that I knew someone, and I pointed the van south.

"Where are we?" asked Annie as I pulled in to Emily's driveway. The frost had finished the last of the hedge roses and withered petals littered the pavement.

"This is my girlfriend's house. She's on vacation, but will be back tomorrow. You should be safe here tonight."

"I didn't know you had it in you to have a girlfriend, Doc," Annie said, as I lugged her suitcase through the back door.

"I didn't either, Annie, I didn't either."

I showed her how to lock the doors, told her to keep the shades down, and not to answer the phone or the door. "There's food in the freezer and in the cabinets. And for God's sake, don't make a mess. Emily's a neat freak."

Annie smiled. "I won't, and I'll be all right. Doc, I appreciate you looking out for me. Nobody else does much. If I can help you sometime ..."

"I know you will, Annie. Now, lock the door. I'll be back with Emily tomorrow afternoon."

***

I drove home, ate a can of soup, and made some calls. Bishop has three nursing homes, and Noah Atherton was in the second one I called.

I identified myself as "Doctor Mullins" to the receptionist, and she cheerfully supplied me with Noah's room number. I knew that he had had a stroke, and when I saw him, I knew it was a massive one. His room was darkened and smelled of dead skin. Noah lay on a partially raised bed with a feeding tube stuck down his nose. Waste dripped into a colostomy bag on the side of the bed. I snapped on the bed lamp, and his eyes darted around until they focused on me. He blinked at me a couple of times, which told me that his mind was cognizant.

"Noah Atherton?" I asked.

His eyes blinked once.

I'm Doctor Mullins, Noah," I said. "I found something that belongs to you."

He blinked once more.

I opened the file folder and pulled out the copies of the handbills. I held each in front of his face. "Look familiar, Noah?" I asked.

He blinked twice.

I stuck a couple of rosters at him. "How about these? Got your name on them."

He stared at me.

"I found them, Noah," I hissed close to his ear. "I found the bodies you hid sixty years ago in the old hotel. I know that you killed them. You and your buddies." I stuck two pictures back in his face. "You know them now?"

He blinked once and closed his eyes. I shut off the light and left him to his demented thoughts and with his stink of death.

***

I stopped by the hospital and retrieved the stick lattice from my office. There was no doubt in my mind that Atherton and his Klan killed the six victims in the hotel, and others as well, but I was curious about the lattice and hoped Mrs. Stolmyer would know something about it.

Mrs. Stolmyer's daughter greeted me and escorted me to the living room. She sat as before, with her ankle resting on the matching foot stool.

"Why, hello again, Doctor," she said and raised a yellow and green afghan above her knee. "Look what I got." She tapped her walking cast with her cane. "So much better than that blamed chair. Lorraine," she addressed her daughter, "see if the doctor will join me in a cup of tea. It'll take the chill off his bones."

Lorraine brought a tea set, helped pour, and excused herself.

"I found the Atherton house," I said.

"Good. What else did you find?"

"Plenty. Too much, maybe." I told her about the pictures and rosters with Bird's and the mayor's names.

"So it goes on." She stirred her tea. "Not much different than in my time. What do you think you'll do?"

"I just don't know," I said. "I'm working on it, though."

"I know you are."

I pulled the lattice out of its bag. "Mrs. Stolmyer, I found this in one of the sealed rooms with the skeletons. You see it's all made of sticks. It seems that Atherton had a bunch of these stored in his attic. Do you have any idea what it's for?"

She turned the lattice over in her hands and traced a few of the sticks. Her face lit up. "Why, I think Lulabelle Atherton made these. Lulabelle was Noah's mother and was from the south. Maybe she brought the Klan to Bishop. Anyway, when Noah's father died, I guess money was tight, what with the depression and all. Lulabelle took to making these lattices and decorating then with glass balls and leaves fashioned out of paper. Supposed to look like a grape vine and be a wall hanger. She sold them at church socials and the like. I suspect that they hung in more than one Klan members' house."

"That's it?" I asked. "Just a wall decoration?"

She handed the lattice back to me. "That's it. I don't know why one would have been at the hotel. But it is evidence that someone from the Klan was in that room, isn't it?"

"Yeah, I guess," I said, "for all the good it does."

"Something good will come out of it. I didn't live eighty-seven years without learning that good things can come out of bad. Now help me up. I want to show you how I can walk."

Mrs. Stolmyer hobbled with me to the front door. "Good to be walking under my own power, even if it is slow," she said as I opened the door. "Now, you be careful, Doctor. I'm counting on you to right some wrongs."

Chapter Nineteen

I drove to Des Moines on Sunday under a leaden sky and with flurries of snow kissing the windshield. When Emily disembarked the plane I pulled her to me and held her tight as other passengers swirled around us.

"Jesus Christ, I missed you," I said.

"I missed you, too." She squeezed me back. "Let's get my luggage and go home." Emily shivered next to me in the van. "Goodness, what happened to the weather?"

"It got colder," I said. "A lot of stuff got colder." I told Emily about the Klan, the handbills, Bird, the mayor, Mr. Schmidt, and Annie.

"God, and I was going to tell you about how exciting New York was," she said. "I can't believe it. The Klan right in Bishop."

"Believe it," I said.

"Bill," she asked after a silence, "on those rosters there wasn't ..."

"No, I looked. No Hardens anywhere."

"Thank God. I mean I was sure, but this is just beyond comprehension. I never would have suspected such a thing."

"I know. If someone had told me something like this two months ago, I'd have laughed in his face." I rubbed my eyes. "And I never would have believed that Bird could have been part of them. Never. I've known him all my life. I don't understand how he could do it."

She patted my arm in silent comfort.

Emily was surprised to find smoke wafting from her chimney as we pulled into the drive.

"I told you about Annie," I reminded her.

"Yes, you did. All the other overwhelmed me, and I had forgotten about her. How long is she going to stay?"

"Until I figure out what to do, I guess."

"Well, let's meet her," she said as we walked to the door.

Annie met us in the living room holding the fire poker like a baseball bat. She relaxed and let it swing down when she saw me. "Doc. Jeez, am I glad to see you."

"Annie, this is Emily, the owner of the house and my girlfriend."

Annie crossed the room and extended her hand. She was wearing jeans and a plaid flannel shirt and looked more like a coed than a hooker. "Pleased to meet you," she said. "Thanks for letting me stay here. I started a fire. I hope that's okay. I was so cold."

To my relief Emily smiled. "It's just fine, dear. But I think I'd better get the furnace started if the weather's going to stay like this."

The furnace and preparations for dinner forced the last of the chill from the house. Annie helped in the kitchen, and I was soon presented with a plate of fried chicken and potatoes.

"I missed your cooking, too," I said when I finished my second helping. "That was good."

"Man lives on canned soup and sandwiches," Emily said to Annie. "Anyway, Annie did most of it."

"Yeah? You're a good cook. I think I'll take some of the leftovers for lunch tomorrow."

"You're not going to work tomorrow, are you?" asked Emily.

"It's Monday," I said. "Why wouldn't I?"

"After all you told me about the sheriff and the mayor, how could you be safe?"

"I protected myself pretty well. I don't think they could just gun me down in the ER."

"No, but accidents can happen," said Emily.

"Yeah, but then all the information gets released. I'm betting they don't want that. Besides, I don't want to look like I'm hiding out, scared."

"Well, at least stay here tonight. Then you won't be alone in your house."

"I think I could be persuaded," I grinned.

Emily and I retired early, and Annie settled into the guest room with some magazines. I had sorely missed Emily's touch, and we stroked each other under the comforter. Stroking quickly yielded to unrestrained passion, and our bodies writhed, one trying to envelop the other.

"My God," I said as I cradled her my arms. "This is heaven on earth."

She nestled closer. "Yes. Be careful tomorrow, Bill, and come home to me."

"I will." I hadn't come home to anyone in twenty years.

***

I left for work before five without disturbing Emily or Annie. I got some bacon and eggs from the hospital cafeteria and ate them in my office while I stared at the names on the 1985 roster. Except for Bird's, the mayor's, and Cap Schmidt's, all were unfamiliar to me. Not a big surprise, I thought, since I only knew a dozen or so people in town. I noticed that behind Cap Schmidt's name a "W" appeared. I recalled that Klan leaders were known as wizards, and I figured that Cap had assumed that position after Noah Atherton's stroke. Just wonderful, I thought, and returned the roster to the file drawer and reported to the ER.

I spent my lunch break in my office looking at older rosters, which only contained more unfamiliar names. I pulled out the pictures of the six victims. Sealed from sight, I thought, their existence wiped from earth. I wandered into the morgue and looked at the body bags, and I knew what I was going to do. I returned to my office and made some calls. My last call was to Emily to tell her I wouldn't be home for dinner.

I wasn't expected at the Schmidt's until seven, and I waited in my recliner. Part of one of Emma's specials and half a glass of brandy sat on my coffee table. I had attempted both, but my mouth was too dry for the sandwich, and my stomach too sour for the brandy. I thought about high school, fishing with my dad, watching Bird uncoil his limbs for a lay up, kissing a girl for the first time, and seeing Paul take a nap in his crib.

"Nothing is ever simple," I muttered and forced a sip of brandy.

***

Mildred Schmidt greeted me at the door and led me to the living room, explained that Cap was in the barn, and offered me a piece of cake. I got down a couple of bites while we chatted about the weather and Paul and Cindy. Cap entered from the kitchen and dropped his hat and coat on the couch. He looked at me, but didn't smile or offer a greeting.

"Mildred," he said, "Bill and I have some business to discuss in the den." He stalked off, and I knew Bird had already talked to him. I thanked Mildred for the cake and followed him.

Cap settled behind his desk and tapped his fanged letter opener. "All right. Let's get to it. What do you think you want?"

"First, I want to know if I'm talking to the right person. You in charge?"

He cocked his head back, and his white hair bounced. "I am the Wizard of the Bishop Chapter, if that's what you mean." His pride was obvious.

"That's what I mean," I said and shifted in the chair in an impossible attempt to get comfortable. "Bird probably told you that I have evidence to link the Klan to those skeletons that were found in the old hotel. Got all your rosters, too."

"So what? Nobody alive had anything to do with those people, except maybe Noah, and I don't think he could be prosecuted. Who cares about the rosters? The Klan's in charge around here. Nobody's going to get upset over a list of names."

"Maybe not," I said. "But the Klan isn't in charge of the rest of the country. And I'm betting that you don't want the world to know that you belong and neither does anyone else on those lists."

Cap tapped his letter opener. "The Klan is going to be in charge of the country someday whether you or anybody else likes it. We have lobbyists, PR men, and our members are working their way into local government positions. You know, school boards, city councils, stuff like that. This is happening all over, and pretty soon we'll get this country set right again."

"Well, all that hasn't happened yet, and your PR guys haven't gotten rid of your negative image, and you don't want the world to know that you belong."

"True leaders aren't always popular. Washington and Lincoln had enemies and were misunderstood. The Klan is just misunderstood right now, but we'll be on top soon, and we'll run this country as it was meant to be. So far you haven't impressed me with your threat of exposure." Cap smiled and fondled the fanged handle.

It amazed me that people involved with the weird, evil, bizarre, or depraved claim to be misunderstood and compare themselves to great men.

"Well, that could be," I smiled back. "But you might be afraid of what all the lawsuits will cost you."

"Lawsuits? What the hell are you talking about?"

"I figured Bird told you. I got the pictures that Noah Atherton took of the dead bodies. I got evidence to place him in the hotel, and I've got a witness." I crossed my legs, feeling more comfortable and confident.

"Yeah, Bird told me some shit like that. What a joke. No court is going to be impressed by that flimsy evidence. Even if they were, who would you prosecute? Noah is the only person around who was alive then, and nobody is going to prosecute him in his condition."

"I was thinking more along the lines of civil court. They hear cases for monetary damages, and they're more lenient about evidence rules than a criminal court. You see, I've already positively identified two of the skeletons and have located one surviving family member, who will undoubtedly want to collect damages. It's just a matter of time before the others are identified and those families will sue as well." I knew there was almost no chance of that, but I figured a little bluff couldn't hurt. "Being a Wizard an' all I suppose you know that the Klan isn't faring very well with those cases. Last time out it cost you over a million dollars. This case would probably make that look like chump change."

Cap drummed the fang of the letter opener in the palm of his hand. I knew he was considering what I said, and I decided to push a little.

"You might also think about the media. This will be a big story, and news people from all over will cover it. You might not realize how persistent and obnoxious these people can be. They'll camp right on your front lawn. You won't be able to fart without them knowing it. And those are the legitimate reporters. Wait until people from those supermarket rags get here. You won't believe the nasty little stories they'll put out about you and your family. Might even involve some of your farm animals."

He jerked his head up a fraction at the mention of family, and I decided to push a little harder. "Won't be long until they find out where Cindy lives. They'll be following her around wanting to know all the perverted things you did down on the farm."

"Your boy is with Cindy," he said.

"Yeah, but his father isn't head of the Klan. I doubt that they'll care much about him. But they'll sure be interested in your daughter."

He sucked at his upper lip and bit it. I made a guess that Cindy didn't know about his involvement in the Klan.

"What do you want?" he asked.

"Just what's fair. The Klan killed them, and the Klan should bury them. I talked to Mr. Riley at the mortuary. He said that for two thousand dollars each he will provide the service, coffins, flowers, limos, and a common head stone. He said he'd donate the expenses for the fetus."

"So you want money after all. What? Twelve thousand?"

"No, actually I want fifty thousand."

"You're out of your mind. What's the rest for? Blackmail?"

"No, it's for the surviving family member, and it's way less than any court would award. Even less than your attorney fees."

"Still a lot of money."

"Yeah, but I know you can get it. All I've been hearing lately is how big and powerful the Klan is. Raising fifty thousand should be child's play for you."

"What do we get in return?"

"Everything I know stays under wraps, and you can continue your lives of hate and terror."

"How about we get those photos and other evidence?"

"Nope. I figure you guys might hold a grudge, and I want to live a little longer. It's my insurance policy."

"How do we know you aren't going to use them?"

"You got my word."

"Your word. Ha. That's not much."

"Maybe not, but that's what I'm giving you."

Cap drummed the fang on his palm a few more times, then opened his desk drawer and dropped it in. He replaced it with a revolver and pointed it at my chest. "I could kill you right now and end this bullshit. Bird wouldn't touch me."

I gripped the arms of the chair and willed my voice steady. "Yeah, you could kill me, but then everything would go public, beyond Bishop County. Bird might not touch you, but he's not the law all over the country. Despite what you claim, the Klan is not running everything yet, and both you and Bird would have your asses in prison."

"We can ruin you in this town," he muttered.

"Ruin what? My practice? I don't have one. You want to

keep people from coming into the ER? Fine, I get a salary and a damned little one at that. I don't have much you can take away."

"You got a house and a car," he said.

"Yeah. And anything happens to them and the file goes public."

"You got a son," he said with a smirk, and he tapped the butt of the revolver on the ink blotter.

The smirk pissed me off, and I was out of the chair and put my face into his face. "And you got a daughter. Anything happens to Paul, even a goddamn bad headache, and your daughter is going to know the cowardly slime that she has for a father. That he reigns terror on innocents while hiding under a sheet. Think about how she's going to deal with that. I'm tired of dicking with you. This is the deal. I get a call from the bank by noon tomorrow saying that you want to deposit fifty thousand dollars into my account or I start releasing information. The fifty grand keeps everything under wraps unless anything happens to me, my family, my friends, or my possessions. Be smart, Cap. I can play hardball, too."

He pushed himself from my face and slapped the fang on his hand. "You're pissing me off now. You don't want to do that."

"I don't give a shit if you are pissed off. Try to do something to me. I don't care. Just remember the world is going to know who you are and what you do. And for all your stinking pride, all that shit about serving the community, you bastards are still afraid to let anyone see under your sheets. You can't let anyone know who you are because it's too damned shameful. You can't even tell your own daughter." I reached across the desk, grabbed the arms of his chair, and jerked him close.

I felt him try to pull away, but I held fast, and he stopped struggling. "Tomorrow, noon, or your filthy little secret gets on the six o'clock news." I gave the chair a push, propelling him into his trophy wall and walked to the door, hoping to Christ I wouldn't be shot in the back.

CHAPTER TWENTY

I told Emily what had happened as I sipped brandy by her fireplace. The second glass began to warm me and stopped my hands from trembling.

"Bill," she said when I finished. "Either you're one of the cleverest men I know or one of the stupidest."

"I've done so many stupid things in my life; I hope that I was smart for once."

"I guess we'll know by noon, tomorrow." She stroked my cheek. "I hope you were smart, too."

Time crawled the next morning. I was certain that I had been far too aggressive with Cap, and expected each patient to reveal himself as a Klan member and attack me. Noises startled me, and I dropped equipment. By mid-morning Rosalee suggested that I medicate myself.

The call arrived at ten minutes to twelve; Cap had let me dangle as long as possible. The assistant manager of the bank informed me of the deposit of fifty thousand dollars to my account, and indicated that I could pick up the receipt or have it mailed. I thanked her and phoned Emily to tell her that, at least so far, I wasn't stupid.

I made four stops on my way to Emily's house. At the bank I had a cashiers check made for twelve thousand, and I put thirty-two thousand into a new account. I presented the check to Mr. Riley at the mortuary, and arranged for services on Friday. I asked Ervin to print an obituary that I had prepared and to announce the funeral services in the *Reporter*. Finally, I stopped at my house to pack some clothes to stay with Emily. I told myself that it was to make her feel safer, but, in truth, Bishop, my home, frightened me.

Emily hugged me at the door, and I told her about the funeral arrangements. Annie was in the kitchen preparing dinner, and I showed her the passbook with the thirty-two thousand dollar balance.

"This isn't a princely sum, Annie, but it's your money," I said.

"What?" she asked. "Why are you giving me money?"

"Actually, I'm not. The Klan is compensating you for the loss of your great-great aunt."

Annie stared opened mouthed for a moment. "You mean you got the Klan to give me money?"

I nodded.

She laughed. "This is great. The Klan giving money to a black girl."

"There are some stipulations on the money. First, you have to use it for your education. Go to Des Moines or Omaha or Sioux City and find a good school and learn to be a dental assistant, day care operator, cook, beautician, or whatever you want, with a plan, maybe to open your own shop. Hell, be a lawyer or a doctor, even. Second, to get the money you have to write to me and tell me what it's for. That way I know I'll hear from you. And third, no more tricks."

Annie hugged my neck, and I felt some wetness. She released me and wiped her face. "Thank you. I don't really understand why you're doing this, but thank you. I don't know if I can ever repay you."

"Do what I said, and I'll be happy."

She nodded and retreated with her passbook to the guest room, and I joined Emily on the couch in the living room. "That was nice," she said. "And generous. Why did you do it?"

"I'm not sure, exactly. I kind of like Annie, and she hasn't had much of a chance in life yet, and maybe her great-great aunt dying like that somehow affected her life before it started. Besides, it wasn't my money, and it should go for something good."

"You provided a lot of caring treatment for that patient, Doctor," Emily said.

"Yeah, I guess I did."

"That's a good sign," she said and put her arms around me.

***

The funeral was tasteful and attracted more people than I'd thought would attend. Mrs. Stolmyer attended, and hobbled, assisted by her daughter, to the front row of the mortuary chapel. Annie, who decided that her great-great aunt should remain with her eternal companions, sat with Emily and me in a middle row, and Rosalee and Emma settled behind us. Ervin, who was clad in a black suit with a red PRESS button on the lapel, occupied a rear seat. A few elderly people who I didn't know were scattered around in other seats.

Mr. Riley had decorated the chapel entirely in white, including the flowers, coffins, and linen skirts. This was at the request of Father Finley, the local Catholic priest, who offered the service. In his sermon he explained that the white represented hope and peace. He alluded to the fact that the seven were victims of hate and violence, but through their sacrifice we, the living, might find peace, and in that peace, tolerance for all people. He compared them to St. Stephen, who he said was stoned to death for preaching about Christ, and who is considered the first martyr for Christianity. The seven, he said, were Bishop's first martyrs who, like St. Stephen, gave their lives to spread peace.

I thought that Father Finley's words were cogent, and I found some comfort in them. If the people of Bishop could find peace and tolerance, the seven would not have died in vain. I looked at the smattering of Bishop's population in the chapel and knew that the Klan, with its philosophy of hate and prejudice, still had a grip on most of the community. I realized that achieving peace and tolerance would take time, maybe generations, and effort.

Mr. Riley had borrowed hearses from surrounding mortuaries, and we made an impressive procession down Main Street on our way to the cemetery. Since Annie was the only known relative, she was afforded the limousine with Father Finley; Emily and I followed them in my Mercury, and the others trailed behind us. As we passed the Dairy Queen, I noticed Bird's long figure propped against his patrol car's fender. His head wagged as he followed each hearse and car. His face was impassive, and his arms were folded across his chest, and I was unsure if his presence signaled a threat, his guilt, or was simply a coincidence. When we entered the cemetery gates, I glanced into the rear view mirror to see if he had followed us. He hadn't, and I felt a mixture of relief and disappointment.

The cemetery was on the west side of the lake and involved three rolling hills that were basically unsuitable for agricultural purposes. We drove nearly to the top of the third hill where I could see a white wreath and some chairs next to a covered mound of dirt. Emily accompanied Annie, and I assisted Mrs. Stolmyer. When I settled her into a chair she gripped my hand and pulled me close. "I don't think I've felt this good in years," she whispered to me. "Now, don't you give up, Doctor."

The graveside service was short. Father Finley called our attention to the inscription on the common stone, which said, "United by Death, but Remembered by the Living," and admonished us to be cognizant of the sacrifice of the seven victims. He read the standard passage that ended with, "Ashes to ashes; dust to dust. We commend our brethren to the Lord," and Annie threw the symbolic shovel full of dirt onto the coffins. Father Finley blessed us, and people moved to their cars or into small groups for subdued conversations. Annie and Emily were in such a conversation with Father Finley, and I walked slowly around the grave. Despite the cold weather the day was exceptionally bright, and I could see the light glistening on Lake Bishop's surface in the distance.

I had nearly become mesmerized by the glints of light on the water when I felt a hand on my shoulder. I started and turned. "Oh, Father. I enjoyed your sermon. Thanks for doing it," I mumbled.

"It was my pleasure," said Father Finley. "I understand that we have you to thank for this ceremony. What you did took a great deal of courage."

"Well, thanks," I said, and started to move away. I knew what he was referring to, and it made me uncomfortable.

He put his hand on my arm before I could get away. He was years older than I, and his gray hair was cropped close to his head. The chill had made his cheeks red and accented the broken capillaries beneath his skin. He had shaved closely, and he had a clotted nick under his left sideburn. His hand was large compared to his frame, and it held me firmly. "Doctor, this is a small town and what you did is no secret. But remember this: you are not alone and have no need to be frightened. Careful, yes, but not frightened." He released my arm and reached into his cassock, produced a pack of cigarettes, and offered me one. I shook my head, and he lit himself one and blew smoke through his nose. "I'm at St. Mary's. Come see me, and we'll help each other help Bishop." He gave me a pat on the shoulder and walked to the limousines with smoke streaming behind his head.

***

By Christmas, Bishop was continually swathed in blankets of snow. Its whiteness was broken only by the plowed roads that etched an occasional dark line and by the shadows of the snow-laden trees. Emily and I celebrated the event at her home, and Paul and Cindy joined us for dinner. Paul had saved half of his tuition for the spring semester, and I provided him with the other half. Cindy would graduate and had been offered a temporary position as a third grade teacher in Waterloo. Marriage was planned when Paul graduated. I hadn't told Paul about Cap Schmidt, and I didn't know if I would. I don't know if children bear the sins of their fathers; I hoped not.

Annie left for the Quad Cities after the funeral and enrolled at Blackhawk Community College and is studying radiology. She writes twice a month even if she doesn't need money. In her last letter she said that she'd had a date with a classmate. It was her first real date. They went bowling.

Bishop and I have settled into a truce. I report to the ER

every day, tend to my patients, and have an occasional sandwich at Emma's. Cap Schmidt ignores me, and I am not on a first name basis with the mayor anymore, but Bird waves when I see him; I wave back; some parts of your life never go away. I've moved into Emily's house, and mine is for sale. Emily and I have talked about marriage and relocating. The marriage seems set for the spring, but the relocation plans are in the more distant future and may be determined by where I can start a private practice.

I met one snowy evening with Father Finley. We sipped brandy together by a bay window in his rectory and watched the snow smooth the edges of the outside world. He talked about the Klan and said that he had worked against it since he had been assigned the Bishop parish, but that his work had mostly consisted of providing comfort to its victims. He said that to his knowledge I was the first person to confront any Klan member in Bishop. That inspired him to intensify his methods, and he founded an organization called Klanwatch, which did exactly what its name implies. It records any criminal activities that involve Klan members and attempts to expose any Klan affiliations of political candidates. He had written to their headquarters in Montgomery, Alabama, about Bishop's Klan and my conflict with it. They wanted to send a representative to Bishop to organize an anti-Klan movement. Father Finley suggested that I meet with that representative to help get the movement started. I agreed, maybe because I had finished my second glass of brandy, or maybe for other reasons.

After all, Bird had always said I should be in charge of something.